"I like you, Zac."

The way he let go of her hand, the uncertainty on his face, showed that he knew exactly what she meant. But when he replied, there was no trace that he understood the admission she'd just made. That she wanted him.

"I like you, too, Allie."

Maybe she should just leave it at that. Then she saw the pulse beating at one side of his brow.

"I meant…I *like* you. I know it's not going to come to anything and that you'll be leaving soon. I just wanted you to know that it's the first time I've thought of anyone in that way for a long time."

He smiled slowly, laying his hand on hers again. "Is this all right, though?"

Holding hands? "Yes, it's really nice." Suddenly it felt as intimate as a kiss.

"And this?" He raised her hand, then stopped when it was just a few inches from his lips. Allie caught her breath.

"Yes."

His lips brushed her fingers, his gaze holding hers in the most delicious of embraces.

Dear Reader,

This is my fortieth book for Harlequin, and I'm thankful to everyone whose encouragement and help have brought me this far. If I've learned one thing, it's that the more I write, the less I seem to know!

This wasn't an easy book to write, as it covers some of the issues surrounding image-based sexual abuse. I'm particularly grateful to the editorial team at Harlequin for providing the support framework that makes tackling real-world topics possible.

And my heroine, Allie, and my hero, Zac, have an opportunity for romance, too. Thank you for reading their story.

Annie

ONE SUMMER
IN SYDNEY

—

ANNIE CLAYDON

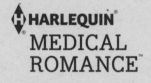

HARLEQUIN®
MEDICAL
ROMANCE™

Recycling programs
for this product may
not exist in your area.

ISBN-13: 978-1-335-59490-7

One Summer in Sydney

Harlequin Enterprises ULC
22 Adelaide St. West, 41st Floor
Toronto, Ontario M5H 4E3, Canada
www.Harlequin.com

Printed in U.S.A.

Cursed with a poor sense of direction and a propensity to read, **Annie Claydon** spent much of her childhood lost in books. A degree in English literature followed by a career in computing didn't lead directly to her perfect job—writing romance for Harlequin—but she has no regrets in taking the scenic route. She lives in London, a city where getting lost can be a joy.

Books by Annie Claydon

Harlequin Medical Romance

Dolphin Cove Vets

Healing the Vet's Heart

The Best Man and the Bridesmaid
Greek Island Fling to Forever
Falling for the Brooding Doc
The Doctor's Reunion to Remember
Risking It All for a Second Chance
From the Night Shift to Forever
Stranded with the Island Doctor
Snowbound by Her Off-Limits GP
Cinderella in the Surgeon's Castle
Children's Doc to Heal Her Heart

Visit the Author Profile page
at Harlequin.com for more titles.

To Soraya, with thanks for wise thoughts
and encouragement.

**Praise for
Annie Claydon**

"A spellbinding contemporary medical romance
that will keep readers riveted to the page,
Festive Fling with the Single Dad is a highly
enjoyable treat from Annie Claydon's immensely
talented pen."

CHAPTER ONE

A TWENTY-FOUR-HOUR JOURNEY. As they'd flown over the baked heart of Australia, it had occurred to Dr Allie Maitland-Hill that if she wasn't far enough away from London yet, there was nowhere else left to run.

The thought made her feel *more* determined, rather than less. When the news had first broken at the hospital, whispers turning into rumours, and then firmed up by a bland official announcement that had given precious few details, Allie had run to Hampshire for the weekend. Two days tramping the countryside with Aunt Sal had always fixed whatever life had thrown at her, but this time it hadn't even come close.

On Monday morning she'd returned to work to find that the hospital had made another announcement, this time with further details. The online group, where members had posted pictures and videos—Allie's blood had run cold with panic at the thought of videos—was no longer a suspicion but a reality. Several of the ringleaders had been identified and immediately suspended. They weren't named, but James wasn't there when she'd happened to pass his work station at the hospital and it had lain empty for the whole week.

The following weekend, she'd tried to run a little further. Surely Yorkshire would do what Hampshire had failed to accomplish? But two nights in a hotel, most of it spent in her room looking out at the glorious view and trying to think of an alternative to the one possibility that was boring its way into her heart, had been fruitless.

James had been affable and charming, almost shy, but he'd left her under no illusions that he was interested in her. Allie had liked the gentle three-month courtship that moved slowly from looks and smiles towards a coffee date and then an evening meal together. She'd ignored the veiled hints she'd heard from a friend that he wasn't all that he seemed, because everyone else who knew him seemed to like him, and he'd never pressed their relationship to go any faster than it should.

When they'd spent the night together he'd seemed so perfect. He'd pulled back the bed-covers, keeping the lights on, because he said that he wanted to see everything that passed between them, and they'd made love for hours.

He'd called her the next day, seeming genuinely upset. They'd had a wonderful time together but he had a lot going on right now, and couldn't take things any further. He'd been vague and uncharacteristically thoughtless, but Allie had swallowed the questions that had come to mind and put it down to experience. James had said that he'd always remember their time together with fondness, and then hung up.

As she'd sat miserably in her hotel room, Allie had wondered whether James had more than just fond recollections to remember her by. Maybe he had an aide-memoire, to recall their time together, that she didn't know about. The thought had eaten away at her, like corrosive acid, and when she'd returned to London she'd called the confidential hotline that the hospital had set up for anyone with concerns that images of them might have been shared without their knowledge.

That had been eighteen months ago, now. Time spent facing the truth and not running from it. Finally Allie had buckled under the pressure and decided she needed a change. Some anonymity where she didn't feel that everyone knew what had happened and where she was constantly wondering who had seen what on the internet. When she'd gone to her line manager to tell him that she was giving up her job, he'd suggested an alternative. Dr Zac Forbes had been in Sydney for the last two years, as part of an exchange scheme between her own hospital and a sister hospital in Australia. His tenure was due to finish soon, and since there were currently no suitable candidates to replace him Allie's application could be pushed through quickly. She could keep her job in London open, and return without losing any seniority.

And Australia could be a new start. Or—it was impossible to run any further without going into space. Whichever way Allie was minded to think about it, it had seemed to open up options for a future that increasingly seemed to offer very little, apart from just getting through the day, and then surviving the night.

In a daze of weariness, she followed the line of passengers slowly making their way off the plane, and through customs. Someone had directed her to the meeting area and she'd followed a group of people, just off the plane and clearly looking forward to a reunion with family or friends. Allie watched as they fell into the arms of the people waiting for them, smiling a little at the warmth that escaped the tight circle.

Maybe if she concentrated on that, it would stop her from shivering.

Zac had said he'd be waiting for her here and she summoned up the two-year-old image of him, from her own hospital. Pale brown hair, and…she didn't know what colour his eyes were, they'd never had much to do with each other back in England. Probably some shade of brown, which went with the muted colours he always wore. Perhaps he'd be carrying a placard with her name on it, which would distinguish him from all of the other anonymous faces that surrounded her.

Allie sat down at the end of a row of seats, clutching the handle of her suitcase tightly and scanning the people in the waiting area. She couldn't see Zac; maybe he'd been detained at the hospital… The impulse to flop to one side, curl up on a couple of seats and take a nap seized her and she opened her eyes with an effort, only to see a card propped up against the cash register of a coffee cart. *Dr Alexandra Maitland-Hill.*

Maybe she was supposed to ask there where she was supposed to go next. Then the man who had just paid for coffee picked up the disposable cup along with the card with her name on it and turned. Zac…?

There was nothing anonymous about him.

This was a man who met someone's gaze, a lot broader across the shoulders than she remembered Zac, his hair kissed blond by the sun and his skin golden. He wore a pair of casual trousers, along with a dark blue T-shirt emblazoned with a brightly coloured design on the front. Something about him reminded her of the shy, gentle man that she remembered, whose only two aims in life seemed to be study and merging into the background. But there was a lot that didn't.

Australia had obviously been good to him. Allie automatically raised her hand, waving to catch his attention, and he gave a frank, open smile that made her wonder momentarily whether this really *was* Zac and she wasn't fast asleep on the plane still, dreaming her own version of *Revenge of the Body Snatchers*.

Blue. His eyes were dark blue. And Zac Forbes was absolutely gorgeous.

Zac had thought about this a lot. When the news had broken at the hospital, the police had contacted him to ask whether he knew anything about the abuse that had been taking place and although Zac wished he could tell them something that would be of help, he was also relieved to be able to say that he'd no clue about what had been going on. He'd watched the situation from afar, seen Allie's bravery in coming forward and encouraging others to do the same, and realised the toll that must have taken.

And now he could see it in her face. She was smiling, clearly disoriented at finding herself in a strange place with precious little sleep, and no one could be expected to come off a long international flight looking completely self-possessed. But there was more. A drawn watchfulness that she probably didn't even know that she was exhibiting. He'd hardly recognised the bright, bubbly woman that he remembered from two years ago.

And now her bravery and what Zac assumed must be a wish for a new start had carried her here, and he'd made up his mind that he would make this transition as painless as possible for her. It was up to him to provide as much security and success that he could for her during their five-week handover period.

He sat down next to her, leaving one seat empty between them. 'How was your flight?' Zac decided that sticking with obvious questions was probably best at the moment.

'Fine…good.' She answered too quickly for that to be anything other than a pleasantry. 'I could do with some fresh air.'

He nodded. 'Would you like a coffee before we get going? We can take it outside.'

She hesitated. Zac wondered whether she'd lost the ability to trust in the simple offer of a drink. Too late, the thought that any drink might be spiked occurred to him, and it tore at his heart that this kind of precaution might be the first and most important thing that occurred to Allie these days.

Then he saw a flash of the bright warmth that he recognised from two years ago. He'd always felt a little envious of her carefree, outgoing spirit, and Allie's sudden smile made his heart lurch in his chest.

'Yes. Thanks, that would be nice. Unless you have to be somewhere?'

'I'll be dropping in to the hospital this afternoon, but there's no rush. We've plenty of time.' He got to his feet, and Allie strung the strap of her handbag across her shoulder. 'Let me take your case.'

One more thing that she had to think about. Allie was clearly apprehensive and feeling vulnerable in an unfamiliar place, but she was making a determined effort to return his overtures of friendship. The impulse to protect her, to tell her that he'd do everything and anything to keep her safe, made his heart ache.

'Thanks.'

There was a trace of reluctance as she pushed the large case towards him, and Zac picked up her cabin bag, propping it on the top and then waiting for Allie to get to her feet before he started to walk over to the coffee cart.

'Um…' She was scanning the list taped to the front of the cart, frowning. Zac searched his memory and coffee with milk popped out from one of the creases of a past that he'd thought he had carefully folded away.

'A flat white is somewhere between a cappuccino and a latte. Frothed milk without the foam.' He grinned at her.

'That sounds good.' She reached into her bag, fiddling with a zipped pouch inside, and Zac handed her a ten dollar note. He'd been in the same place two years ago, picking a random brew from a list and sorting through the bundle of unfamiliar notes he'd got from the bank in England.

'Thanks.' She examined the note and then grinned at him, the dark shadows under her eyes seeming to disappear for a moment.

Such beautiful eyes, wide and brown, shot with gold when she turned her face towards the light. Allie's dark curls and her smile had always brightened his day back in London, even if approaching her to talk about anything other than work was out of the question.

He had to stop this. Wanting to make Allie smile meant that he had to get close to her.

And he guessed that getting close would be a whole new challenge after all that she'd been through. He'd made up his mind to make her welcome, and do as much as he could to give her a safe place to live, while she was finding her feet here. He really needed to stop thinking about the feeling in the pit of his stomach that he wanted to roll back everything that had happened to Allie in the last two years, and somehow make it all go away.

After the air-conditioned hum of the plane, the sounds and smells of the open air began to dispel the fog that had formed in Allie's mind. She could look around her and drink in her surroundings, a cup of coffee in her hand, Zac sitting quietly next to her. She took off her hoodie, turning her face up to the warmth of the sun. Everything seemed brighter somehow, and clearer.

'I think I'm going to like it here.' Allie decided that since this *was* a fresh start, she should be optimistic.

'I do. There's something about moving to the other side of the world that gets everything into perspective.'

Did he know? It wouldn't be beyond the bounds of possibility, he must have friends back at the hospital, although Zac had always seemed too busy with his books and his work to socialise much. Allie rejected the thought. Fresh start. Time to stop wondering what everyone she met knew and what they'd seen on the internet. What they *might* see if it occurred to them to look.

'Did you?' She sipped her coffee, trying to make the question seem casual.

'I think so. A little less work and a little more play. Although there's still plenty of work and a lot to learn.'

Allie had been banking on that. Something to keep her mind occupied, and to tire her out so that she might sleep. Right now she was more interested in the leisure side of Zac's metamorphosis, because work was something that was always there, both here and at home. And the change in him was even more marked now that they were in the open air. He seemed relaxed and so at one with the world around him.

'What do you do? In your spare time.'

He chuckled, stretching his legs out in front of him. 'Well… I've learned to surf.'

'Surfing! So you're a real Australian now, are you?'

'Nah. Still noticeably English. Ask anyone at the hospital.' He shrugged. 'I hear that Cornwall's good for surfing.'

'So when you get home you'll be driving down there for weekends?'

'Who knows. I may well give it a go.' He spun his coffee cup into a nearby recycling bin, and Allie yawned behind her hand. 'Do you want to get going?'

She nodded. 'I could do with a couple of hours' sleep. Then hopefully I'll make it through the afternoon without dozing off and sleep tonight…'

Zac had put her luggage in the back of a rather battered SUV, which seemed to fit perfectly with his new persona of a man who liked to spend time at the beach. He'd held the door open, frowning awkwardly and brushing a few specks of sand from the seat before she got in, in a nod to the shy, apologetic man who she'd thought would be picking her up at the airport. In a place that seemed so like home in some ways, and so different in others, contradictions might be something she ought to expect.

They drove for half an hour, along free-flowing highways and then through residential districts, with houses set back from the road and shaded by trees. Finally, Zac turned onto a coastal road.

'You live here?'

He smiled. 'Cronulla's handy for the hospital,

it's on the same side of Sydney. And it's only half an hour by car, or an hour by train from the centre of town if you want to go out for the evening.'

Going out. Two years ago, Allie would have been up for that. But she couldn't remember the last time she'd been on an evening out, now. Handy for the hospital would be good, though.

'And it's by the sea.'

'Yeah. And not too far from the Royal National Park, if you want to go walking or cycling.'

She hadn't done much walking or cycling recently either. Or been to a beach, although the deep blue of the sky, merging in the distance with the water, did seem inviting. Allie would settle for the privacy of four walls, and some peace and quiet in which to sleep right now. That vision seemed to disintegrate a little as Zac turned in to a covered parking spot, next to a brightly painted shop front.

'You live above a surf shop?' She couldn't suppress the note of surprised disappointment in her voice as she got out of the car. Zac definitely hadn't mentioned *that* in their brief set of exchanged emails.

'I'm friendly with the owners. They used to live above the shop but they have a growing family now, and they need a bit more space.

Don't make any judgements just yet—wait until you see it…' He took her suitcase from the boot, then ushered her along a path that led around the side of the building, to a set of steps that led up to a first-floor doorway. He pulled his keys from his pocket, unlocking the door and standing back to let her step inside.

The curtains were drawn against the morning sun, and the place was fresh and cool. Wooden floors and neutral colours gave the feeling of even more space to an already huge area by English standards, which combined a kitchen and living room. Everything was neat and gleaming, and Allie could see none of the personal items that made a place look lived in.

'I've packed up my stuff and put it all in the spare bedroom.' Zac was hanging back, clearly waiting for Allie's verdict.

'You didn't need to do that…' Suddenly she was glad that he had. Accepting his offer to live here while she found her feet had seemed like a sensible thing to do, but Allie had already decided that finding her own space was her top priority. But staying here for a while didn't seem quite so challenging as she'd thought it might be.

'It's very quiet.'

Zac raised his eyebrows. 'You're expecting to have to fight your way through a throng of beach bums sipping beer to get to the front door? Mark and Naomi sell high-end surfing equipment so the place doesn't attract that crowd. You won't find them holding any midnight beach parties either, they have young children.'

'That's a relief. It seems really nice here.'

He smiled suddenly. 'You haven't seen the best part yet.' Leaving her suitcase by the open doorway, Zac strode across to the full-length curtains and pulled them back.

Allie caught her breath. There were sliding doors leading out onto a large shaded balcony, with chairs and a small table. And beyond that the sea, with views of a curving, wooded peninsular to one side. Suddenly the neutral tones of the room made absolute sense, because who needed colour and decoration inside when there was the animated beauty of the panorama outside?

'It's gorgeous, Zac!'

He nodded, seeming to relax a little. 'The view's actually better from upstairs. And it's never quite the same two days running.' Zac turned as a woman's voice sounded from the doorway.

'Knock, knock!'

'Hey Naomi. Come in.'

The woman standing in the doorway stepped inside. She was about Allie's age, with blonde hair and golden skin, and was carrying a baby in a brightly coloured wrap. A little girl of about four stood next to her, holding a large bunch of flowers.

'Hi.' Naomi grinned at Allie. 'We just popped in to say hello and to welcome you.' Naomi let go of the little girl's hand, and she ran to Zac.

'Hey, Izzy.' He squatted down on his heels in front of the child, and she pushed the flowers into his hands. Zac chuckled, leaning towards her, speaking in a stage whisper. 'They're beautiful. But I don't think they're for me.'

Naomi chuckled. 'No, they're not, you can go and pick your own flowers, Zac. Izzy, give them to Allie.'

Izzy snatched the bunch of flowers back, and walked over to Allie. Despite the ache in her back, Allie bent down towards the little girl. 'Hey, are you Izzy? I'm Allie.'

'These are for you. Welcome to Australia.' Izzy proffered the bunch of flowers.

'Thank you, Izzy. They're so pretty.'

Izzy nodded. 'That one's waratah…' She pointed to the lavish, dark pink blooms, bound together with dark green foliage. 'I helped pick them.'

'You did? You chose such nice ones.' Allie smiled at Naomi. 'Thank you so much.'

'Waratah's the floral emblem of New South

Wales.' Naomi gave her a bright smile back, beckoning to Izzy. 'We won't stay, you must be exhausted, but I just want you to know that if Zac's not around and there's something you need, my husband Mark or I are always downstairs during the day. Our house is at the top of the hill right behind here, so I hope you'll pop in for coffee some time.'

'Mark and Naomi's place is the one with the waratah bushes,' Zac interjected.

'Yep. And before I forget—Zac's lease is up in six weeks, but you're welcome to stay as long as you want after that. If you like the place we can sort out a lease, or if you'd prefer somewhere different feel free to stay on a weekly basis while you're looking round.'

'Thank you. That's really kind of you.' Allie was beginning to feel that her feet were really back on solid ground again. Naomi exchanged a wordless smile with Zac and Allie wondered whether he'd had something to do with the plan.

'It's our pleasure to have you here.' Naomi grabbed Izzy's hand. 'Zac, why don't you go and bother Mark in the workshop? I expect Allie wants some time to herself to settle in and catch some sleep.'

'No can do, I'm afraid. I said I'd pop in to the hospital for a couple of hours. If he's still there when I get back, I'll catch him then.'

'He'll be there, he's got a lot to do.' Naomi gave a smile and left them alone.

Allie was finally feeling that she was grinding to a halt. Zac had put the flowers in water, saying she could arrange them later, and carried her suitcase upstairs. The bedroom overlooking the sea had the same balcony and panoramic views, and it was cool enough to be able to sleep. Zac snapped the front door key from his keyring and handed it to her.

'Why don't you take it? You'll need to get back in again when you return from the hospital, won't you?'

'I won't disturb you. I'll be over in Mark's workshop if you want anything. Just put your head around the door downstairs and Naomi will point you in the right direction. Dinner at six?'

'That's fine. I just need to close my eyes for a few hours.'

Zac nodded. 'I'll leave you to it.'

He turned, walking downstairs, and Allie heard the front door close behind him, suddenly realising that she was breathing a sigh of relief. Alone. In a room that had been stripped of all his belongings, with just empty fitted wardrobes and freshly laundered sheets on the bed. And her fingers closing around the front door key, which meant she could let down her guard.

Did he know? Had he done all of this to give her some space and make her feel safe? Allie wasn't sure how she felt about that, or whether she should feel an echo of that humiliation she'd felt at the hospital in London, where everyone knew. She was too weary to even think about it.

Allie stumbled into the en suite shower room and then changed her mind. Sleep first. She closed the curtains, making sure that there were no chinks that allowed the outside world to intrude, then sat down on the bed, looking around her. There was a thumb turn for a bolt, under the handle of the door.

No. She was making a new start and she didn't need to do that. She should take off her clothes, lie down and sleep, like any other normal person. All the same, she walked over to the door, turning the stiff bolt back and forth a couple of times so that it engaged more easily, and then locked the door.

CHAPTER TWO

ZAC RETURNED TO the apartment at five o'clock to find that Allie was already showered and dressed, the flowers arranged neatly in a vase from under the sink. From the carrier bag that lay on the kitchen counter, she'd clearly ventured out for ten minutes to the newsagent.

'Anything happening?' He gestured towards the newspaper that was spread out on the breakfast bar.

'I can't tell. I'm not sure who all the people in the headlines are yet.' She smiled at him impishly. A few hours' sleep and she was clearly feeling a little more in charge of the situation, and Zac reckoned that might be exactly what she was aiming for.

'There's a place by the hospital where you can order the English papers if you want them.'

She shook her head. 'I'm in Australia now.'

Right. So she was serious about making a new start. *Really* serious—even Zac hadn't gone to those lengths. He supposed that it mattered what a person was trying to leave behind. His own demons had been intensely personal, but Allie's had been bound up with the hospital authorities and the courts, and ultimately the newspapers.

He prepared dinner and after they'd eaten Zac suggested they take a walk. Allie was interested in everything, questioning him about his life here and the things that she saw. They talked and joked together, but the one thing that wasn't discussed was the thing most on his mind. The one thing that seemed to dictate everything she did.

Allie said that she was ready for an early night, and Zac sat downstairs, watching the moon rise across the sea, unable to stop himself from listening to the quiet sounds of her moving around upstairs. The almost imperceptible sound as the bolt turned on the bedroom door...

He tried not to take that personally, telling himself that Allie had probably bolted the door when she was alone in the apartment. What kind of humiliation led a person to even think of bolting the door to their bedroom, to give them the courage to lie down and sleep?

Zac sighed. He knew something about humiliation. He'd said nothing about his own parents' jibes when he was growing up, resorting to the

safety of books in an attempt never to meet anyone's gaze. He'd found his own space, and now
it was time to give Allie the space she needed.

After a restless night, Zac decided that getting
up at six on a Saturday morning was preferable to staying in bed thinking about things
he couldn't change. He'd weighed up all of the
pros and cons—his suspicion that Allie wanted
a fresh start and wouldn't be happy about anyone here knowing what had happened back in
England, against the idea that she'd already
been treated dishonestly and the first thing she
needed from him was the truth, even if she
didn't much like it.

Early Saturday mornings were usually spent
putting in a couple of hours' surfing, but Mark
had things to do today before he opened the
shop. Zac couldn't work up much enthusiasm
to go alone, so he made coffee and went out to
the balcony, staring out over the deserted beach.
When he heard movement in the kitchen and
turned, he realised from the clock on the wall
that he'd been sitting there for an hour.

'Good morning. How did you sleep?'

'Like a log. It's so quiet here.'

Yes, it was. If you kept the sliding doors that
led out onto the balcony closed. Zac preferred
to open them and fall asleep to the sound of the

sea, but he supposed that was a small pleasure that Allie couldn't allow herself.

'Would you like some breakfast? There's bacon and eggs in the fridge, or toast…' Allie's slim figure was accentuated by the T-shirt and Bermuda shorts she wore this morning, and he could see that she'd lost weight.

'Bacon and eggs *and* toast? And coffee?'

He grinned. 'Coming right up.'

Setting to work, Zac filled two plates with eggs and bacon, and a third with toast, while Allie made the coffee. They sat at the breakfast bar and he realised that his appetite wasn't quite equal to the task in front of him, although Allie was tucking in hungrily.

'Will you be sorry to leave?' Allie pushed her plate away and picked up her coffee mug. 'You seem really settled here.'

Zac had thought about it. 'It's time I got back to London. I'm not looking forward to the winter, though.'

She nodded. 'You have things to do back home?'

He nodded. Zac had his reservations about going home but at the same time he needed to make that journey. When he'd left England he'd been looking for something that he now felt he'd found. Going back was the final step in reclaiming the man he'd become.

'Not quite. It's more…things to rediscover.'

She was clearly considering what that might mean. He should say what he had to say now, before worrying about it tore a hole in him. Try to reassure her that even if he couldn't completely understand what she'd been through, he'd fought his own battles, and he knew how tough it could be to leave the past behind.

'Allie, there's something I wanted to mention.' Now he *couldn't* go back…

She turned to him, a flash of alarm showing in her eyes. Suddenly she seemed very small and frail, and Zac wanted to reach out and protect her.

'It's just… These last two years have been good to me in a lot of ways. I had to get away and do some major reassessment.' Just saying it was harder than he'd thought it would be.

'You seem different. More at home with yourself.'

It was nice that she'd noticed. And since he was about to tell Allie that he knew all about what had happened to her it was only fair to stop using generalisations about what had happened to him. He'd made up his mind that he was going to be honest, and so his next step should be obvious.

'I spent most of my childhood being bullied by my mother. My father as well, although he wasn't around much. My reaction to that ended up being my escape. I buried myself in my books and got to university.' Zac was staring at the grain of the wooden breakfast bar now, and with an effort he turned to meet Allie's gaze.

Her reaction hit him like a blow to the chest. Allie's eyes were dark and wide with shock, her cheeks flushed. And there was a look of not just concern, but real pain on her face.

'I'm so sorry, Zac. I wish…' She shrugged. 'I wish I'd known that you were going through something like that.'

He shook his head. 'I was determined that no one should ever know, or be able to reach me, and I'd had plenty of practice in keeping it a secret. Allie, I'm only telling you this because I've had a chance to make my peace with what happened while I've been here. I know what happened to you and…'

The expression on her face, and the way she seemed to shrink away from him without really moving, silenced Zac. Allie's cheeks were bright red now.

'I wondered if you'd heard. I suppose you're still in touch with friends at the hospital.' She seemed utterly miserable, suddenly.

'I guess I might have been if I'd been that close to anyone there. I was actually contacted by the police, and I had to go down to the station in Cronulla and answer questions from the investigating officers in London by video link.'

Her hand flew to her mouth. 'They thought you had something to do with it? That's crazy.'

'They had to speak to everyone who'd worked at the hospital. I'd only been gone for six months and presumably the whole thing had been going on for longer than that.'

'I meant…' She pressed her lips together. 'I would never have thought you'd be involved in something like that. Even if I have proved my judgement's not particularly sound at times.'

Two contrasting emotions almost knocked him from his seat. The rush of warm gratitude that Allie thought him incapable of the kind of crime that had hurt her so was followed by the chilling realisation that she thought that some failing on her part had contributed to what had happened to her.

'We're all capable of being deceived. And we're all capable of feeling ourselves to blame for things that aren't our fault.' He could attest to the latter.

She nodded, clearly not really believing him. 'Thanks.'

'Allie, all I want to say is that I know what it's like to want to make a new start. It happened for me, and I believe it can happen for you. And… I just want to be honest with you and to make sure that you get whatever space you need right now.'

'Does anyone else know?' A tear rolled down her cheek, and she brushed it away impatiently.

'I haven't spoken of it to anyone. I didn't think it was my place to then, and it certainly isn't now. And no one's mentioned it to me in our discussions about the handover period.' Zac wondered if people here *did* know and they were just keeping quiet about it.

'I was going to hand my notice in, and my boss persuaded me to come here instead. He said that what had happened wouldn't be discussed with anyone here and even though I'd waived my anonymity to make a plea for people who might be affected to come forward...' She seemed to choke on the words, but Allie fanned her face with her hand, pressing on. 'It was some time ago. I doubt anyone will put two and two together.'

Clearly Allie was *hoping* they wouldn't. His own uncertainty, the worried examination of every conversation that he'd had with anyone for the last two weeks, was something that Allie had been living with for a long time now. It felt as if he was peeling off the layers, finding a different possibility for hurt in every one.

'I'm sure you're right. The exchange programme is intended to share medical expertise, and in my experience there's no interaction concerning anything else. It's for you to decide who knows what.'

That was clearly something of a relief to Allie and she reached across and took his hand. 'Zac, I really appreciate…everything. I don't quite know what to say…'

'Nothing's always an option. You could always leave it at that until you do have something to say.'

Happiness was beginning to eat away at all of Zac's uncertainty, all of his fears about going too far, or maybe not far enough. All he needed right now was to feel her hand in his.

Allie gave a teary smile, squeezing his fingers. 'That's a really good thought, Zac. Shall we take our coffee out onto the balcony and decide what to do today?'

There was always something not to like, even in the most perfect housemate. Allie had had her share of navigating those waters when she'd first gone to London to study, and when she'd finally been able to put a deposit down on her own place it had been heaven. Going home, shutting the door and being able to just exist in her own environment.

She was still looking for the thing not to like in Zac. He was easygoing, he'd given her a room to call her own and he was a great cook. And he'd set out the terms of their relationship right from the start. He'd told her that he knew about what had happened to her back in England, and even thrown in a little of his own experience, so that she didn't feel too much like a project in vulnerability. Back in the day, when she had a full social schedule she'd appreciated the solitary refuge of her own home at times, but Zac seemed like that one in a million that you'd actually want to come home to.

And he was horribly easy on the eye as well. When she'd come downstairs this morning and seen him sitting on the balcony, an exercise in relaxed harmony with the world around him, she'd caught her breath.

There had been a time she'd know just what to do about that. Get to know Zac again, find out all the ways in which he'd changed and see where that led them. Allie knew just what to do now too. Stay away, because absolute trust was far too great a gift to risk giving anyone.

But it was the weekend, she was in a new place and she could go as far as enjoying his company. A supermarket for the weekly shop wasn't the most enticing of venues but Zac had said that his stocks of fresh food were running low.

Their first stop was at a small market that

dealt in tropical fruits. Allie chose dragon fruit, because she'd never tried it before, and they came away with several paper bags filled with the kinds of things you'd never see in the shops at home. The supermarket had a more familiar range of foodstuffs, but Zac seemed to be in no particular hurry, dawdling after her with the trolley as Allie inspected everything carefully.

'Why did you get that one?' He'd thrown a packet of breakfast cereal into the trolley.

Zac shrugged. 'It's the one I always get. I used to eat it back in England.'

Allie inspected an unfamiliar brand. 'This one's got raisins and less sugar. I might try it.'

He grinned, removing his own purchase from the trolley. 'I'll join you then. It would be a shame to leave without having tried the full gamut of Australian breakfast cereals.'

He was joking, and Allie smiled with him. If different brands and unfamiliar fruit were about as far as she was prepared to go in terms of trying new things right now, then at least they might get her into the habit.

'What made you come to live here?' The place seemed to suit him so well, but she couldn't quite imagine the old Zac fitting in so seamlessly.

'I was living in hospital accommodation for starters—I dare say they offered you a room?'

Allie nodded. She'd weighed it up against Zac's offer and reckoned that the risk of living with one person she knew was probably less than that of sharing accommodation with a group of strangers.

'The hospital units are nice, but I can't really recommend it long-term. I was desperate to get a place of my own, so I made up a checklist and started touring around the different neighbourhoods in Sydney. There are a lot of great places that are closer to the centre of the city, and ex-pats tend to gravitate there because there's plenty to do and a thriving nightlife. Places like The Rocks or the North Shore.'

'I'm not really looking for nightlife at the moment.' Two years ago Allie would have been spending her free time making new friends and seeing new places. Now, she just wanted somewhere to escape the incessant chatter, and the constant worry that some of it might be about her.

'Yeah, they didn't tick all of my boxes. Cronulla's quieter, a bit more relaxed and more residential. It's considered quite a long commute into the centre of Sydney so a lot of people who live here work locally. When I came here I made a detour through the Royal National Park, and then drove down to the beach and took a walk. That was enough to fall in love with the place, and I went to the real estate agent and got a list, then came down the next weekend to take a look around. I saw the rental sign up at the surf shop downstairs and popped in to ask about it, just for comparison's sake really.'

'And you ended up taking it?'

Zac smiled, reaching for some gravy browning, and then put the packet back onto the shelf, waiting for Allie to choose.

'Naomi showed me the apartment, and I really liked it. There's such a great connection with the outside…' He glanced at her, and Allie nodded. She knew what he meant; the barrier between outside and inside didn't seem to exist. That had made her very grateful for the comfort factor of closely woven curtains in her bedroom.

'I asked what they wanted for the place, so Naomi left Mark to deal with the customers and collected up Izzy and we went down onto the beach to talk terms.' Zac grinned. 'Apparently I passed the Izzy test.'

It made sense that one of Naomi's first priorities would be to find someone who'd be child-friendly, and Zac's quiet, gentle nature would have been in his favour.

'What was the Izzy test?'

'I make good sandcastles. The moat cinched the deal; Izzy loved it. And Naomi made me an offer I couldn't refuse.'

'Which was…?' From the look on Zac's face, Allie reckoned she wasn't going to manage to guess it.

'She threw in a paddleboard. She said that I couldn't live so close to the sea without having some kind of beach equipment and guessed—quite rightly—that I hadn't brought anything of the sort with me from London. The morning after I moved in, she appeared at the front door and told me that we were going down onto the beach to try it out.'

Allie laughed. 'That's nice.'

'Yeah. It wasn't so nice when I fell off it for the fourth time, but I got the hang of it. That was what prompted me to try surfing. At this time on a Saturday morning, the beach is usually beginning to fill up and Mark and I are sitting outside the shop drinking coffee, after a couple of hours out catching waves.'

'I thought you said that the shop didn't attract any rowdy elements?' Allie smiled up at him and Zac chuckled.

'I'll be back in London soon, so it's not an ongoing problem…'

They called in at the shop after they'd put the shopping away, and Allie was introduced to Mark, who shook her hand and asked her if she could swim. Zac waved him away laughingly.

'Give Allie a chance to get her feet back on

the ground before you try to get her onto the water, eh?'

'I can swim.' Allie exchanged a smile with Naomi.

'I can swim too!' Izzy declared, tugging at the hem of Zac's T-shirt, clearly wanting to be included in the conversation. Zac lifted her up and she wrapped her arms around his neck, clearly happy to be on the same level as the adults.

'Yeah, you're a mermaid, aren't you? Your mum says that you swam before you could walk.'

Naomi chuckled. 'Yes, she could. And before Mark notices that you've admitted to being able to swim, Allie, I'm going to make a cup of tea. It's time for a break, we've been busy this morning.'

'I showed a man a surfboard.' Izzy piped up.

Mark smiled. 'Yeah, that's the ticket, Iz. He wanted a tin of wax, but I expect he'll keep your choice of boards in mind for the future.'

'I'll leave you here to help Dad, then.' Naomi jerked her thumb towards the baby bouncer. 'Zac, you take Finn outside and find a place in the shade, and I'll make the tea.'

CHAPTER THREE

JUST AS ZAC was beginning to think that Allie was beginning to relax and settle into watching the world go by from the small shaded area in front of the shop, the call came. Bad timing. But then the timing was infinitely worse for the people who'd been involved in the accident…

'I'm sorry…' He drained the last dregs from his cup and then got to his feet. 'Got to go to the hospital. There's an emergency.'

'One of your patients?' Allie gave him a questioning look.

'No, there's been a bus accident. There are a lot of people coming in to the ED—that's A&E—and they need some help to deal with everyone.'

'I'll come.' Before Zac could shake his head in reply, Allie stood up.

'Are you…officially on the staff?' He wondered what the position was with that, and guessed that Allie might find herself sitting waiting for someone to sort the necessary paperwork out before she was allowed to see any patients.

'As of last week. I signed everything, and video-conferenced with HR before I came.'

'Really?' Zac's eyebrows shot up.

'Allie's just told you, Zac.' Naomi frowned at him. 'Will you go already?'

Fair enough. Naomi was less protective of Allie than he was, and maybe he should stop treating her as if she was about to break into small pieces. She might be vulnerable, but she'd showed a lot of strength too.

'You're a lot more efficient than I was.' He murmured the words as he backed the car out of its parking spot, and Allie gave a grim chuckle.

'Not really. I did it so that I wouldn't chicken out of getting on the plane at the last minute...'

Allie hardly looked around her as they hurried into the hospital and through to the Emergency Department. She'd clearly retained the same focus when it came to her work, and Zac privately admonished himself for wondering if that would be the case. There was no way that the hospital in London would have allowed her to come here if her work had suffered.

He steered her over to where Beth Kramer, the head of the ED, was directing everyone to the right place, keeping the atmosphere busy but calm. She smiled when she saw Zac, beckoning him over.

'Thanks for coming, Zac.'

'No worries. This is Dr Allie Maitland-Hill, she's my replacement from London.'

'Are you officially employed here yet, Allie?' Beth dispensed with the introductions and got straight to the point.

'I signed everything and spoke with HR—Joe Simmons,' Allie replied.

'Okay, I'll have to give him a quick call at home, just to make sure everything's in order. You understand ..?'

'Of course. I just want to help if I can.'

'Great. Over your jet lag?'

'I'm fine.' Allie's firm answers seemed to reassure Beth, and she nodded.

'And your specialty?'

'Paediatrics, the same as Zac.'

'Good. Zac will sort you out with some scrubs and anything else you need.' Beth glanced at him and Zac nodded compliantly. 'By the time you're ready I'll have spoken to Joe, just to make sure there's nothing outstanding, but I'd like you to work with Zac this afternoon if you would. I have no doubts about your abilities—'

'Thanks.' Allie waved away Beth's explanations. 'Since I'm new, I'll need someone to tell me how everything works here.'

By the time they returned, Allie wearing a set of scrubs that one of the admin staff had found for her, Beth had everything sorted. She beckoned to an ambulance crew who had just arrived, pointing to one of the cubicles and murmuring to Zac to, 'Get on with it, then.'

As he led Allie to the door of the cubicle she grinned at him, almost stopping him in his tracks. There she was. The old Allie, who met every challenge head-on and did her absolute best for every one of her patients. He'd watched her from afar, back in London, admiring her confidence and her ability to connect with people. She was no different now, and he shouldn't assume that she was vulnerable in every area of her life.

'Don't take it personally that Beth wanted you to work with me…' He stopped by the door of the cubicle as the ambos wheeled their patient towards them.

'Why should I? She's just being sensible. Medicine's medicine, but I was told to expect a few differences in admin and procedures here.'

Zac nodded. He'd reckoned that her first day might cover those, but since Allie was being thrown in at the deep end here, there wasn't much opportunity for that. 'I'll stick to the admin and procedures then. Let you get on with the medicine?'

The amused look in her eyes made his stomach lurch. Something that resembled the normal interplay between a gorgeously attractive woman and a rather starstruck man. 'You can help with the medicine if you like.'

He chuckled. 'Okay, thanks.'

The ambos wheeled the trolley bed into the cubicle, and quickly gave Zac a status report on their patient. He'd been travelling with his mother, who had also been injured, and had been brought here. It looked as if she'd broken her jaw, so they couldn't get any information about the child from her, but he'd told them his name was Billy and that he was five years old. They suspected concussion and a broken ankle. Billy had become increasingly drowsy in the ambulance, but had initially been complaining that his head hurt, and he seemed bothered by the light.

'Where do you want me?' Allie would understand this was a vote of confidence. Zac didn't make gestures that might compromise the welfare of a patient.

'You take his leg. I'll see if I can rouse him and check on his reactions.'

Zac nodded. Good choice. If the boy was going to respond to anyone's smile it would be

Allie's. He set about carefully removing the temporary support that the ambulance paramedic had placed around the boy's leg.

'What do you see, Zac?'

'I think the ankle's fractured, but the skin's not broken and it doesn't feel displaced. Should be reasonably straightforward. You?'

Allie puffed out a breath. 'I don't know. Something's wrong…'

Zac glanced at her. 'You think he may have sustained a TBI?' Traumatic Brain Injury was always something to watch for after an accident, and in a bus the passengers might well have been thrown around.

'Maybe… I don't know. I don't see any signs of injury to his head, and his pupils aren't dilated, even though he seems drowsy and unresponsive.' She puffed out a breath and then seemed to come to a decision. 'Zac, is his leg all right for the moment? I think we should order a CT scan, but I'd really like to just see if it is possible to get any more information from the mother.'

'Sure. I'll put the scan into motion. There's a board by the nurses' station that shows who's in which cubicle, or you can ask Beth. She always knows exactly what's happening.'

'Great, thanks.' Allie hurried from the room and Zac pulled his phone from his pocket, to check on how soon Billy could be sent for a CT scan.

She was gone for a while, and Zac was about to call a nurse to see if they could find her when Allie reappeared in the doorway.

'Where have you been?'

'In the next-door cubicle. The mother's jaw is definitely broken, and I had to ask yes and no questions. But it seems that Billy was sick before the crash. The nurse with her said that the bus that crashed goes straight past the hospital. She was bringing him here to see a doctor.'

'So...' Zac thought quickly. 'He's pale, difficult to wake, the ambos said he was complaining of a headache and seemed photosensitive.'

'A rash...?' Allie beat him to the next question and Zac nodded.

Carefully they sat Billy up, taking off his T-shirt and examining his skin. 'Here... Look.' Allie lifted Billy's arm, and Zac saw a group of red pinpricks on the boy's side.

'You were right. This looks like meningitis.'

'So we'll do a blood test and get ready to start him on fluids and broad-spectrum antibiotics?'

'Yes—I won't cancel the scan, there's still a chance he may have bumped his head in the crash, and it would be good to check that the infection hasn't caused any swelling around the brain.' Allie was nodding in agreement and

Zac smiled. It was always good to find a doctor who seemed in tune with his own thoughts, and when that doctor was Allie it felt even better.

'Shall I go and see if I can get more details from the mother? I think if I give her a pen she may be able to write her answers down.'

'Sounds good. Could you ask Beth to find a nurse and send her in, please?'

'Will do...'

It had been a busy afternoon. Billy's mother had refused any treatment other than analgesics until she'd told the doctors all she knew about Billy's condition before they'd arrived at the hospital, and Allie had spent a while at her bedside, gathering information from her. Zac had stayed with Billy, monitoring him carefully and expediting his treatment, until he was transferred to the children's ward.

He joined Allie at Billy's mum's bedside, and was able to reassure her that Billy was having treatment and seemed to be responding well. Only then had she allowed her own doctors to come anywhere near her, and Zac had practically had to drag Allie from the room as a nurse sat down beside her bed, taking her hand.

Then there were cuts and bruises, sprains and a broken wrist, as the doctors worked their way through the patients with less serious injuries.

Beth appeared in the doorway of the cubicle. 'Time to go home, people. I can't thank you enough, but we've got this now. Get lost, both of you.' She turned to Allie. 'Good to meet you, Allie. I hope I have an opportunity to work with you again.'

As Beth abruptly turned away, already focused on the next thing she had to do, Zac nudged Allie. 'That's about the highest praise you'll ever get from Beth, you know.'

Allie smiled up at him. 'I got that. I'm feeling it.'

She'd shown no sign of fatigue all afternoon, but as they walked out of the hospital together Allie seemed to tire suddenly. She sat in the passenger seat of the car, her eyes closed, and when they reached the apartment she fell asleep on the sofa.

When Zac prepared something to eat, and gently touched her shoulder to wake her, she sat up with a start. He pretended not to notice, and fetched the plates of sandwiches and fruit from the kitchen, setting them down on the coffee table.

Allie leaned over, inspecting the fruit. 'This is the dragon fruit?'

Zac nodded. 'Try it.'

She reached out, picking up one of the chunks of fruit and inspecting it carefully and then tak-

ing the tiniest of bites. This was a world away
from the confident doctor who was able to
think outside of the box and make a diagnosis
that went against everything that the situation
seemed to suggest.

'What do you think?'

'I'm...not sure. Perhaps it's an acquired taste.'

'Yeah, I guess so. Would you like some tea?'

'Some of the herbal tea we got this morning
would be nice, thanks.' She seemed suddenly
listless, staring at the sandwiches as if she was
wondering what to do with them. Zac knew she
must be hungry, they hadn't eaten since breakfast.

But when he returned with the tea she seemed
to have rallied and had picked up a plate and
was tucking into the food.

He sat down, taking a sandwich from the
pile. 'Bit much to ask, really. You've only been
in the country for thirty-six hours.' He floated
the idea.

'It was good. I don't do time off all that well
these days. I like to keep busy.'

Keeping busy until she dropped, in the hope
that she wouldn't have nightmares? Zac decided
not to suggest the idea. 'If you want to keep
busy, I'm going to call Mark and see if he's
going to catch some waves first thing tomorrow.

I could always bring the paddleboard along, in case you decide to try it out.'

She seemed to be turning the idea over in her head. 'What time?'

'Just get up whenever you wake, and look out of the window. If we're there and you feel like it then come down and join us.'

'You make it sound so simple.'

Sometimes things *were* simple. He'd been agonising over his motives—whether his protectiveness towards Allie was strictly down to his horror at what had happened to her, or whether he was beginning to care for her on a completely different level. The two could co-exist—quite separately—as long as he concentrated on acting on the first, and ignoring the second. Allie needed a friend, and wanting to become a lover felt as if it was a betrayal.

'You're very quiet.' He felt her elbow nudge at his ribs. This easy friendship that was developing between them suddenly seemed far too precious to put at risk by wanting more.

'Yeah. I guess I'm tired too. Early night, I reckon.'

Allie stifled a yawn. 'Sounds like a plan.'

Maybe it was sheer fatigue and jet lag. Maybe that she just felt safe here. But Allie had only woken with a start once during the night, and even then she'd managed to relax and go back to sleep. When the first strands of light began to filter through the curtains she got out of bed, showering and dressing before she let the morning in by drawing the thick drapes back.

She could see two figures on the beach, one dark-haired and dark-skinned, the other sun-blond and golden. Mark and Zac both wore board shorts with short-sleeved rash vests, which she'd seen on sale in the shop and were designed to protect them from sun and water. And she couldn't take her eyes off Zac.

Watching while he didn't know it. More precisely, *ogling* while he didn't know it. Her first instinct was to turn away, but something about the way he moved, the way that he seemed so confident and at home in his own skin made her open the sliding doors and step out onto the balcony. Zac was on the beach and he didn't care who saw him. Maybe he didn't much care that the thoughts running through her head at the moment centred largely on how it might feel to touch his golden skin.

All the same she waved, calling to him to announce her presence. Her voice must have been drowned in the crash of the ocean, but something made him turn and he lifted his arm, waving back. This she was allowed to enjoy. An innocent wave and a smile, with hundreds of metres of clear space between them. Even if it did feel wholly intimate.

He was walking up the beach now, leaving Mark behind with the surfboards. Moments of sheer pleasure, when she had every reason to watch every move he made.

You could give a girl a break, Zac. Walk a little slower.

'Are you coming down?' He'd reached the empty road that separated the surf shop from the beach.

'I can see from here.' All she really *wanted* to see, anyway. Surfing she could take or leave.

'Fair enough.' He began to turn away and Allie's heart sank. Maybe being out on the beach, where it was natural to want to feel the sun on your skin and for people to watch each other, wasn't so confronting at this time in the morning. Maybe being with Zac would mean that the feeling of freedom, which seemed to leak out of him, would rub off on her.

Then he turned back. Walking across the road, he came to stand under the balcony, the sun shining in his hair. 'You don't want to go paddleboarding?'

She did, but there was one problem. 'What do I wear?'

'As long as you're comfortable and you don't mind getting a bit splashed, you can wear your best dress. What you have on will be fine.' He gestured towards her shorts and T-shirt. 'Sunglasses probably, and plenty of sunscreen...'

'I thought you said you fell in four times on your first go.'

'Yeah, I did. But I'm not Naomi, I don't think it's funny to rock the board and tip the newbie into the water. And I've borrowed her lifejacket, just in case.'

'In case of what?' Allie was already going paddleboarding, but having Zac persuade her to join him was just too delicious for words.

'Uh... We get a few giant squid around these beaches at this time of year. They'll swallow you in one but they don't like the taste of neoprene, so they might throw you back in if you're wearing a life jacket.' Somehow Zac managed to keep a straight face, and Allie nodded sagely.

'Okay, that sounds like a good precaution.'

'It's a lot safer here than jumping into the Thames...' This time he did betray a smile. He must remember the day when the group of newly qualified doctors had jumped into the Thames in fancy dress to raise money for charity. The scheme hadn't been as reckless as it sounded, they'd chosen their spot and taken precautions against infection, and Allie had thrown herself into the water with joyous gusto.

'I didn't see you there...'

'No, that's because I wasn't. I'm not quite as adventurous as you.'

Zac was clearly beginning to get what so few others did. That *being* hurt and anxious didn't make her a hurt and anxious person. He didn't have the air of someone who was stepping on eggshells around her, and Allie was grateful for that.

'Okay, you're on. Give me ten minutes to get my sunscreen and stilettos on.'

He laughed. 'No stilettos. I'll go and inflate the board.'

Allie would have liked to have watched him walk back down onto the beach again. Compare the back view with the front. But she was too eager for the beach herself, and she hurried inside to grab her sunscreen from the en suite bathroom.

CHAPTER FOUR

THE AIR WAS fresh and warm, the ever-present breeze from the sea ruffling her hair. A perfect morning for the beach, but then Allie imagined that there were a lot of perfect mornings for the beach here. Mark was looking thoughtfully out to sea and Zac had taken the paddleboard further up the beach, to where the water seemed a bit calmer.

'Hey, Allie. Ready for your first dip?'

'Zac said I wouldn't be getting my hair wet.' Allie grinned back at him.

'Right then. I'm sure you won't.'

Allie wrinkled her nose. 'Don't try to put me off, it's not going to work. Can't we do it here?'

Mark shrugged. 'You could, but it's a bit choppy for a first outing. The first really good beach break of the summer has formed just here, you see it?' He indicated the line of higher waves, which crashed onto the shore.

'They move?'

'Yeah, the sandbanks shift, and they may last a few days, or maybe a week.'

'So the same beach can be different?'

Mark nodded. 'That's why I like it. Zac's shifted up a bit to get out of my road.'

Allie was beginning to feel guilty about that. 'Am I keeping him from this…uh…?'

'Good beach break?' Mark supplied the correct terminology. 'No, you're not. Well, you are, but it appears that Zac would rather be paddle-boarding this morning.'

That sounded as if Zac found her company preferable to the waves that Mark found so absorbing. But since Mark's attention was back out to sea, she probably wasn't going to get a solid answer out of him. Allie contented herself with letting the idea form and roll around in her head for a moment.

'I'd better go and see what he's up to then.'

'Uh huh…' Mark was still engrossed in the waves. 'Oh, don't forget the life jacket, it's in my bag. The pink one.'

'Okay. Thanks.' Allie left him to his deliberations, finding a fuchsia-pink lifejacket in Mark's bag and then walking along the beach towards Zac.

'It's bigger than I thought it would be.' Allie surveyed the board.

'This is a two-person board, it's Mark and Naomi's. They take Izzy out on it. Ready to go?'

'Definitely. How do I get on?'

'Just follow me…' Zac picked up the board, walking down to the shore with it, while Allie followed, trying not to think about strong shoulders. She liked strong shoulders on a man, and she liked Zac as well. Coupled with a sunny morning and a crystal ocean, this was getting to be a perfect storm of enjoyment.

Walking out into the water, he stopped when they were knee-deep and set the board down, showing her how to get on to the front of the board and then sit down. That was easy enough, and Allie felt the board dip a little under his weight as he got on behind her. The board started to move forward as Zac paddled away from the shore. Further along the beach, Allie could see Mark, carrying his surfboard into the water.

'You want to stop and see how he does?'

'With the beach break?' Allie decided to show off her latest piece of jargon. 'Yes please.'

Zac chuckled, sitting down on one side of the board, his legs dangling in the water. Allie shifted carefully around to sit next to him.

'See, he's paddled out, and he's ready to catch the next wave. If he gets it right…' Allie saw Mark gain his footing on the board, travelling fast across its peak, and then suddenly he and the board parted company and Zac let out a groan.

'Where is he? I can't see him…'

'He's okay. There, look.' Zac pointed to where Mark was swimming strongly for the beach, the board towed behind him.

'He's going to try again?'

'What do you think? He'll try until he gets it right.'

'So this is what you do out here in the mornings. Falling off your boards until you get it right?'

'More or less. I'm not as good as Mark is, so I've been known to give up on the tricky ones. Mark just keeps going.'

'The waves aren't quite as big as I thought they'd be.'

Zac raised his eyebrows, laughing. 'It's not always a matter of size. What Mark's doing isn't easy.'

Mark was paddling back out again, and they both watched intently. This time he stayed on his board, riding the wave for its full length. Zac let out a *'Yes'* under his breath.

'Don't you want to go and try it? Mark said that this sandbank was new.'

He turned suddenly, looking at her, so much

warmth in his eyes that it made Allie shiver. 'No, I'd rather be here.'

'But…' The words died, strangled by the lump in her throat. His eyes were as blue as the sea and far more inviting. In that moment, everything that a man and a woman could possibly do together seemed just a word away.

A word that she was too afraid to say. What if all the things that had been taken from her couldn't be claimed back again? Those private moments that had been shared with the world felt irretrievably spoiled. If she tried to experience them again with Zac, would she just relive the humiliation? Would that humiliation be all that he saw if she let him make love to her?

Zac was looking at her speculatively now. 'You want to give paddling a go?'

'It is a paddleboard. It wouldn't be right to come all the way out here without at least trying it out.' Allie breathed a sigh that hovered somewhere between disappointment and relief. This would be a lot easier to handle than staring into his eyes and all of the promise they held.

'Right then. First thing to remember is, whatever you do don't drop the paddle.'

'Okay. That's straightforward. Do I have to stand up?' The gentle rock of the board was soothing when she was sitting down, but if she was on her feet it might be a little more tricky.

'No, that's somewhere around lesson four. You can start off by just kneeling, like this...' He carefully moved to demonstrate, showing her how to move the paddle.

'Okay. I can do that. Let me try...'

Allie *had* dropped the paddle, when she'd become a little too enthusiastic and lost her balance, almost falling off the board. Zac's arm had coiled around her waist, steadying her, but before she'd had a chance to shiver at the deliciousness of feeling him so close he'd drawn back again and slipped into the water, swimming to recover the paddle before it was borne away by the waves.

'Try again.' He climbed back onto the board. Zac wasn't afraid to push her, to encourage her to try something one more time and get it right.

'Like this?' Allie tried again and this time something clicked into place and the movement felt right.

'Yes, exactly like that. That's great. Do you want to take us back to the beach, or are you getting tired?'

Allie's fingers curled tightly around the paddle. 'I'm not tired. Show me how to get us back.' She'd achieved something this morning, and it was the first time in a long time that her battles hadn't been all about simply getting through the day. She wasn't going to give up now.

'Okay, it's easy. Let the movement of the waves do all the hard work, and concentrate on steering...'

It had turned into a good day. No—a great day. Zac was beginning to get a feel for where he should back off and when he should push Allie, and something had clicked between them. A kind of closeness which felt right. Just as long as he didn't think too much about where it might lead.

But there hadn't been too much opportunity for thinking. Naomi had joined them on the beach with Izzy and Finn, and Mark had gone back to the shop to open up. Weekends were their busiest time, and when Naomi had seen three cars draw up in the forecourt she'd left Izzy with them on the beach and taken Finn back up with her to help Mark.

'How do you feel about a trip up to the Royal National Park this afternoon?' Izzy had finally managed to expend enough energy to tire her out, and Naomi had taken her and Finn home for lunch and a quiet time. 'There's a nice little pizza place on the way.'

'Sounds good. Is it cool?' As the beach had

filled up, the sun had been climbing in the sky and this afternoon promised to be hot.

'You get air-con with your pizza and...' He shrugged. 'Forests are pretty shady places.'

Allie grinned at him. 'What are we waiting for?'

They'd eaten and then driven to the edge of a thickly wooded area of the park. Zac had stopped the car, letting Allie choose one of the paths that wound into the thickly forested valley floor. She set off, clearly keen to explore.

They wound their way past tall trees and the giant leaves of lush plants, all of which had been unfamiliar to Zac when he'd arrived here. He'd wanted to bring her here because the giant proportions of this place never failed to instil a sense of peace.

'These plants...' Allie was looking around her, drinking everything in. 'They're so big. It's how I imagine a prehistoric forest might be.'

'It's pretty impressive, isn't it.'

'Wonderful. It makes me feel very small. The ocean and this forest.'

'There's more than just forest here. There are lakes, coastal areas and mangroves, along with rocky plateaus on higher ground. I'm not sure you ever could see it all.'

This was a start, though. They walked for a while under the high canopy of the trees, slowly falling under the spell of a world that was far removed from their everyday lives.

'Do you mind…if I ask you something? I'm not expecting an answer.' Allie had seemed deep in thought and suddenly she looked up at him.

Zac thought he knew what the question was, and fully expected to answer. 'Sure. Go ahead.'

'You seem… You *have* changed from the person I knew in London.' She smiled up at him. 'How did you make that journey?'

He could see why the answer would be important to Allie. It was important to him as well. There had been hints and scraps of information dropped along the way to one person or another, but Zac wasn't sure he'd ever said it all in one go.

'Bit of a long story.'

'This seems like a place for a long story. If you want to tell it.'

Yeah. Suddenly he wanted to tell it very badly.

'My parents were…different. My father was a pilot and he was away from home a lot. I suspect he didn't make much effort to change that state of affairs. My mother stayed home and… she kept the place immaculate. No mess, nothing out of place. Now I know that she was exhibiting signs of an obsessive disorder, but when

I was a child all I knew was that the house was cold and pretty scary.'

'Scary?'

'I got very good at staying under the radar. If I made a mess or damaged anything then I was punished for it. She locked me in my room for two consecutive weekends once, because I'd been ambushed by a gang of kids from my school, who smeared some mud onto my uniform.'

'Zac, I wish I'd realised. I'm so sorry.' He felt her fingers graze his arm as Allie reached out to him.

'I know that you spoke out about what happened to you, and I admire your courage. I never did that, even as a child. I knew that my way out was to study and get to university and when I left home I thought that I was finally free. Of course things don't quite work out that way. As you know.'

'Yeah.' Allie shot him a wry smile. 'You can't walk away from yourself.'

'Sometimes a bit of space gives you perspective, though. I went for therapy—probably not enough, but it helped me make a start. I still didn't know how to reach out to the people around me, but I'd at least come to the conclusion that I wanted to live my life differently.'

'Are you in touch with your parents now?'

'There was a fire in the house, when I was in my second year of university. They must have gone to bed and, although the fire never spread upstairs, they both died in their sleep from smoke inhalation.'

'That must have been so hard for you, to lose them like that.'

'It was…confusing.' The complex set of emotions around his parents' death rolled over him, almost as if he was feeling it for the first time. When he looked down at Allie, he saw tears in her eyes. Before Zac could stop himself, with a reminder that this was risky, he'd taken her hand in his.

'Sorry…sorry.' Allie wiped her face with her other hand. 'It should be you that's upset, not me.'

'Don't be, I appreciate the sentiment. At the funeral…' He shook his head, trying to make sense of a day when he should have cried but all he could feel was numb anger and despair.

'You were on your own?'

He shook his head. 'My parents did have family, but they never spoke about them. I only found out about my uncles and aunts by looking them up on a genealogy website. But I reckoned they had a right to know what had happened, and I managed to track them down. Two of my aunts came, the others didn't want to. And one of my tutors from university turned up as well, with his wife. It was a nice gesture. Everyone said all of the right words, how sorry they were, but no one cried.'

Suddenly, Allie reached out and hugged him. She stepped back again immediately, before he could even return the hug, but Zac knew how careful she was of her own space and how much it had cost her. When he'd reached out to stop her from falling off the paddleboard, he'd felt her instinctively flinch.

'I've left most of that behind now.'

Allie looked up at him. 'Not all of it, though?'

There was one thing he'd never spoken to anyone about. But those few brief moments when he'd felt Allie's arms around him had torn down the defences that shielded the most hurtful secret, and now he couldn't hold it back.

'I've never quite been able to come to terms with the broken promises. My mother's idea of punishment was to take things I wanted away from me. If I did something wrong at the dinner table she'd grab my plate and empty my food into the bin. Or I'd be promised something for Christmas and never get it because of something I'd done.' Zac felt a shiver run through him, as if he was physically trying to drive the memories away.

'That's…not something I'd be able to come

to terms with either. Every kid has to believe that they have something that's theirs, which no one can take away.'

Every adult too. Zac had made a rational decision that the abuse that Allie had suffered meant he shouldn't act on the attraction he felt for her. But in a world where anything could be withdrawn, becoming too close to her would also mean he had to face the possibility of losing her.

Not at this moment, though. She'd slipped her hand into the crook of his arm, anchoring him down in a present that could escape the past, and allow the future to look after itself.

'Things are different now…better. I've made a lot of changes in my life.'

She nodded. 'I see them. And you're ready to go home?'

'Yeah. It's important to me to join the pieces of my life back together again—the person who left England and the one who goes back there. Revisit things and places back home and… Does regaining it all on my own terms make sense?'

'I can identify with that.' Allie chuckled. 'Are you still in contact with your aunts?'

'Yeah. We've been exchanging emails and a few video calls. I'm actually really looking forward to seeing them. I'm not quite sure what to expect, but it would be nice to build some kind of relationship.'

She'd understood all that he'd said to her. Being able to explain it all was getting it straight in Zac's head too.

'I really hope you can. It's nice to feel that going back might be a positive step that's in my future somewhere.'

'I'm sorry. I'm talking about my baggage, and that's all in the past now.' Zac had done so in an attempt to be honest and to let Allie know that it was okay for her to talk, but it had turned into something more. Something precious that he felt he could keep.

'You prefer mine?' She smiled sweetly up at him. 'I thought that was one of the things I liked about you, Zac. That you see me first as a person, and only second as someone who's been abused.'

He shrugged. 'That's the way I'd like to be seen.'

The answer obviously pleased her. 'So let's address a more immediate concern, shall we? Do you have any idea about how to get back to the car, or are we going to have to stay here all night and forage for roots to eat for breakfast?'

Zac grinned, pulling out his keyring and flipping the cover on the tiny compass that hung from it. They'd strayed away from the path

while they'd been talking and he'd lost his bearings as well.

'That way.'

She followed the line of his pointing finger,
along a narrow, overgrown pathway. Zac had
to admit that it didn't look the most promising
way to go.

'Okay, we'll give it a try. What's the worst
that can happen?'

CHAPTER FIVE

Zac had to admit to feeling nervous about Allie's first day at work. Not that he doubted she could handle it, but caring about someone brought with it the ability to be nervous on their behalf. Allie seemed to have picked up on his reaction and was exuding confidence.

She'd dressed for success. A plain cream-coloured blouse and skirt, the blouse embellished with rows of buttons at each cuff and a double buttoned fastening at the front, which gave it a unique look. Heels that were just low enough to be comfortable, a little make-up and shining dark curls. The judgement of anyone who failed to be impressed by her might rightly be questioned, and Zac privately added his own, more subjective opinion. She might be laughing on the beach or ready for a business meeting, but Allie was always the most beautiful woman he'd ever seen.

He parked in the hospital car park, and they

went their separate ways. Zac wondered whether
he should have wished her good luck, but doubted
very much that Allie would need luck. All the
same, he contrived to think about her and wonder what she was doing for most of the day.

They met back at his car after work, Allie
looking as fresh and excited as when they'd
parted that morning. The only difference was
that when she got into the passenger seat she
bent down and removed her shoes.

'Been on your feet all day?'

'Not all day. But these shoes are new, I'll
have to wear something a bit more comfortable tomorrow. I got the full tour of the hospital though.'

'And…?'

'It's amazing what you can do with a little
more space than we have available in London.
And good people, of course. Along with good
facilities and a little thought.' She grinned suddenly. 'Great patients.'

That was Allie all over. She never forgot that
the patient was at the centre of everything she
did, and when he'd come in contact with her in
London Zac had been impressed with the way
that she seemed to approach each patient with a
greater than usual knowledge of who they were
and the things they cared about, in addition to
knowing what was wrong with them.

'So you're ready to start work in earnest to-morrow?' Zac was already looking forward to seeing a little more of her than he had today.

'Not quite. The exchange scheme co-ordinator's suggested that I spend this week working with Beth. It gives me a good overview of the continuity between admissions through A&E and onto the wards and Beth wants to carve out some time on Friday to discuss any differences in approach between London and here.' Allie grinned. 'Maybe by that time I'll be remembering to call it the ED and not A&E.'

Good idea. That would help prepare future candidates for the exchange programme and also outline a few of the areas where each hospital might learn from the other. Zac swallowed his own disappointment.

'So you'll be back with the adolescent and young adult team next week, then?'

'You bet, I can't wait. I'm really looking forward to getting to grips with a slightly different balance with my work.'

The team that Zac had been working with for the last two years, and where Allie was due to take over from him, was a little different from the paediatric team at home. It catered for young people from the ages of ten to twenty-four, and there was an emphasis on meeting the specific issues that teenagers and young adults faced when they were in hospital.

'It's challenging.'

She gave him a smile. 'That's what you like about it?'

'Yeah. One of the things. You?'

She nodded, and Zac started the car.

When they arrived back at the apartment Allie insisted on making dinner, although she must have been tired. They took a walk on the beach and he tumbled into bed for an early night, exhausted by a day spent worrying needlessly about her.

Managing his own expectations had been a survival measure when Zac was growing up, proofing him against the promises that had failed to materialise. But it had its good side. When Allie walked into the unit on Friday morning, all he could feel was unexpected and complete pleasure.

'Just visiting?' Spending these few unscheduled moments with her was more than enough to brighten his day.

'Beth's busy today, so we've arranged a sit-down with the exchange scheme co-ordinator on Monday afternoon. Which puts me at a loose end today, so I wondered if you'd mind my joining you for your morning rounds?'

Allie *really* didn't need to ask. 'Yeah, no problem.' Zac decided he could risk being a little more effusive. 'That would be great.'

Bright sunshine wasn't that much of a novelty here, but when Allie's own brand of sunshine was walking next to him it made the day seem warmer. The morning rounds took a little longer than usual because he had to get Allie up to speed with the history of each patient, and afterwards she joined him in a secluded corner of the large food hall for lunch.

'So we've seen everyone now. Apart from Carly. How is she today?'

Zac started guiltily. Carly had arrived on the ward yesterday, and he'd wondered briefly whether Allie had seen her in the ED when she was first brought in to the hospital.

'She was being assessed by Psychiatric Services this morning, and I'm anticipating that their recommendation will be a course of counselling, to start now and continue after she's discharged. There's some concern about permanent disability in her left hand, but I think with minor surgery and physiotherapy we can avoid that.' Carly was eighteen years old and had attempted suicide by cutting her wrists.

'Good. I was worried about that too.' Allie regarded him thoughtfully. 'I was expecting to see her again this morning.'

She always cut to the chase, asking the questions that were the most difficult to answer. Zac had sat alone last night watching the sea, after Allie had gone up to bed, wondering how he might deal with this and coming to no definite conclusion. Zac took a sip of his coffee, trying to clear the lump that had suddenly formed in his throat.

'I had a long conversation with her mother yesterday. Carly's at art school, majoring in photography. She was friends with a guy in the same class as her and they'd go out together on photographic shoots. One thing led to another, they got close and they took photographs of a more private nature. When they split up, he shared all of her photographs on the college's social network.'

'What?' Allie's eyes filled suddenly with tears. 'Why did you wait until now to tell me this?'

'Because I think, given the circumstances, it may be best if you take a step back, and let me continue with her general treatment alone.'

That familiar motion of wiping tears away. Now, more than ever, he realised the fine line that Allie walked between living her life and being dragged down by what had happened to her.

'Don't you think I'm uniquely equipped to help her?'

Zac had anticipated that this would be Allie's first instinct, but he wasn't convinced it was the way to go.

'I know this sounds heartless, but you know as well as I do that we have to retain some distance from time to time, so that we can continue to do our jobs. Compromising yourself isn't going to help anyone.'

'But—'

'I think you should at least think about it over the weekend before you decide.'

He saw a flash of anger in her eyes. 'There's nothing to think about, Zac. The internet group who shared my most private moments, without my knowledge or permission, they took everything from me. They took my trust and my confidence. They locked me up in my flat for eighteen months, afraid to go out and meet people. They took my friends and my home…'

Her cheeks were flushed now, and she was stabbing the table with her finger. Wound so tightly that he thought she might break. Maybe he should have waited until this evening to tell her, but there was no going back now.

'Allie…'

'They will *not* take my voice away. And they

won't take away the oath I made, to do the best I can for my patients.'

'First, do no harm, Allie. We have to tread carefully with Carly, and maybe...' There was no tactful way to say this. 'Maybe you're not ready for this. Maybe Carly's not ready for your anger yet.'

She was still staring at him, her gaze refusing to let him go. But Allie seemed to simmer down a little, leaning back in her seat.

'I'm angry with *you* at the moment, Zac.'

Another challenge. One that Zac wasn't going to back away from.

'Fair enough, I'll take your anger. As much as you want, whenever you want, I thought I'd made that clear.' He hadn't quite anticipated how hard it might be, how much it wounded him to hear Allie say what her life had been like in the last eighteen months, but he'd learned one thing from Australia. You committed yourself and then you rode the wave, wherever it took you.

'*Can* you take it?'

'Try me. One of the reasons I told you about my own childhood was because I wanted you to know that I wasn't going to shrink from what's happened to you. I became an expert in denying what's going on when I was a kid, and I'm not going to pretend that it works.'

She broke the connection between them, looking down at her tightly clasped hands. There was something that could hurt him more than hearing what had happened to her, and this was it.

'Allie...?'

She waved her hand, still refusing to meet his gaze. 'It doesn't matter.'

'Clearly it does.' He lowered his voice, trying to resist the temptation to vent his feelings openly.

Suddenly she got to her feet. Allie left her lunch behind on the table, walking towards the entrance doors to the canteen. Maybe he should let her go.

Maybe he shouldn't. She might regain her cool, but that would just be a first step towards freezing him out. Zac caught up with her outside the canteen, where she'd stopped for a moment, looking around, clearly deciding which way she needed to go. He grabbed her hand, hoping that she wasn't going to protest loudly enough for someone to have to intervene. Kidnapping a fellow doctor was just as much frowned on here as it was at home.

But Allie didn't say a word. She followed him through the busy reception area and out into the sunshine. Zac led her to a secluded spot in the hospital grounds, sitting down on a bench.

Allie joined him, keeping her distance, which was just as well because Zac imagined that a few explosive gestures might be part of the arsenal that she was about to launch at him.

But instead she looked at him blankly. Hiding behind those carefully constructed defences of hers.

'Talk to me Allie. Please.'

'I think you're wrong.'

'Yeah, that's pretty obvious. Can you tell me something I don't know, and change my mind?'

Allie took a deep breath, clearly considering the idea. 'Okay, I take your point. Whatever my reaction to this is, it has to put Carly front and centre. She's the one who's been abused and that makes her the most important person in the room.'

'Along with you.'

'Yes, okay, then. Along with me, because I have to work here.'

At least she'd acknowledged that, and it was the only thing that Zac had wanted to stress. That Allie was here for a reason, and she shouldn't ignore her own well-being. He nodded, deciding that it was about time he stopped making assumptions and listened to her.

'It's all about taking things back, Zac. And the important thing I want to say right now is that you're not one of the people who's made me feel disempowered.'

That really mattered to him. He hadn't always got things right, but he'd tried his best.

'Thank you.'

'I want to help Carly, and I think I can. I think that I can approach her in a way that prioritises how she feels, not what anyone else thinks, and that I can make it clear to her that this is something that's been done to her, and has nothing to do with who she is.'

'I'm not in any disagreement with that.' He ventured an opinion and Allie nodded 'What about you?'

Allie's brow creased. 'You're right, that's something I have to consider and it's more difficult. I'll have to liaise with Carly's counsellor before I do anything, and that means telling them why I think I'm able to understand how Carly feels. Probably a few other people as well. One of the reasons I came here was because I didn't want to be in an environment where everyone knew what had happened.'

'And…?'

'I'll be telling them my own story, from my own perspective. I didn't realise until now how different that feels and how much it matters to me. It'll be hard and I might need a friend…'

She was asking? But the fact that Allie *had*

asked him made Zac feel slightly dizzy. It was the kind of compliment that didn't just slip off the tongue, it came from the heart.

'I'll be there. Probably upsetting you from time to time with opinions you don't want to hear.'

She smiled suddenly. 'That's the deal, Zac. I might upset you from time to time as well.'

But that was okay, because suddenly their relationship seemed stronger than that. He and Allie were both stronger than that, and they could weather a little honest disagreement.

'Yeah. That's the deal.'

They went back to the canteen, expecting that their sandwiches would have disappeared and they'd have to get more. But they were beckoned over by one of the servers, who smilingly produced their plates from under the counter for them, and poured two fresh cups of coffee.

'Thought you hadn't finished yet. Called away?'

Allie smiled at her gratefully. 'Only a minor emergency. Thanks.'

Philippa, Carly's counsellor, had already spent some time with her and decided to allow Carly to get settled into the safe environment of the hospital for a few days, before starting work with her next week. Zac was keeping a close eye on her physical condition and when Allie followed him into her room Carly recognised her from the ED and smiled.

When she admitted that he was right, and it *was* probably best to think everything through over the weekend, he simply nodded as if that had been Allie's idea all along.

She was up early the following morning, and when Zac got back from his Saturday morning surfing with Mark and started to make bacon sandwiches and brew coffee, Allie already had a list of bullet points.

'What do you think?' She slid the paper across the breakfast bar towards him, and Zac leaned over to read it.

'Yeah. Looks good. There's more on the back?' He was holding his greasy fingers away from the sheet, and Allie turned it over for him.

'I like the part about this being something that both you and Carly can learn and benefit from, and that you're not comfortable with doing it without Philippa's advice and support.' His gaze moved from the paper. 'Do you really mean it, or are you just courting her agreement?'

'No! I thought about it, and when my righteous indignation wore off I decided that I was going to need some support. Some clinical support in addition to the friendly support, that is.'

He chuckled. 'Yeah, gotcha. I'll just stay in my friend box, shall I?'

'It's not such a bad box for us to be in, is it?'

Zac was very far from stupid, and he couldn't have missed the way that their relationship had slipped from colleagues to friends to… Something more, that lived in the times when they touched, and when his gaze met hers. When that happened, Zac backed off as suddenly and as often as she did.

'Turn it over again…'

Allie turned the paper back to her initial points and he read them through again, nodding. 'I like your point about not calling it *revenge porn*. I feel pretty uncomfortable when people call it that. It's like asking what a woman was wearing when she was attacked, as if she's done something to warrant a crime being committed against her.'

'Yes, I prefer Image Based Sexual Abuse.'

'Hmm. That sounds more like it. Although, considering the medical penchant for acronyms…' He grinned at her.

'I'll risk it. Do you think I have everything in the right order?'

'No. I think you should put your last points, about being able to reach Carly and your willingness to accept support for yourself, first. That's what you've decided you want to do,

and the rest is important but they're supporting points. At the moment it sounds as if you're
trying to justify what you want, and I think you
need to go in a little stronger than that, and let
Philippa bring up anything she disagrees with.'
He moved back to the cooker, turning the bacon
in the pan. 'Not that I think she's going to dis-
agree, by the way. In my experience, Philippa's
always open to a joined-up approach and a bit
of good sense.'

He managed to make that sound like a compliment instead of an I-told-you-so.

'I appreciate your input. I was thinking of
writing a separate sheet, just noting down what
happened to me. What do you think?'

Zac nodded, buttering the toast before he
turned to face her. 'I think it's relevant. Do you
prefer to write it down or is it easier to talk
about it face to face?'

Allie thought for a moment. 'I could do either.
But somehow writing it down…'

'Gives you a sense of ownership?'

'Yes. That.'

'Well, that's a point you could make as well.
Are you happy to discuss and answer questions?'

'Yes, very much so.'

'Then perhaps that's one of your bullet points.
I think it's a good one, how you take control of

the way you tell your own story.' He grinned. 'Maybe that's one of your introductory paragraphs as well?'

'Yes, that's a good idea.' Allie wrote it down at the end of the list, starring it to go at the top. This felt right. As if she *was* in control of her own story.

'Put that away now.' Zac put her sandwich and a mug of coffee in front of her. 'We'll come back to it when we've eaten.'

CHAPTER SIX

SHE'D RETURNED TO her list, between shopping and cooking, and by the evening Allie was pleased with what she'd done and had typed it all up, along with her account of what had happened to her. Zac had suggested they go out for some fresh air and they'd walked along the beach for a while, sitting down on the sand when the sky began to darken.

'I want you to hear it first, Zac. Before anyone else.'

'I don't need to…'

'But you'll listen, if that's what I want?'

He nodded. 'Of course. I feel honoured that you're trusting me with this.'

Allie took a breath. This was the hardest thing, because Zac's reaction meant more to her than that of anyone else here. And the easiest, because she trusted him better than anyone else.

'James seemed like a really nice person. He was fun, and he seemed very respectful as well.

Sent me little notes and flowers. He didn't push for sex. In fact, I think that was my idea.'

Zac nodded, opening his mouth to speak, and then stopped himself, seeming to think better of whatever he was about to say.

'In the context of what happened next you could call that grooming, but I didn't have any idea at the time.' Allie voiced the obvious, wondering if that was what Zac had been about to say.

'Yeah. Flowers can be just…nice. I guess that's the problem, isn't it. Nice gestures become weaponised.'

Allie let that go. She'd stared at the bunch of waratah that stood on the table next to the sofa, wondering if she might have enjoyed it a little more if it didn't remind her of James. Zac didn't need to know that Naomi's gesture wasn't appreciated quite as much as it should have been.

'What I didn't know was that he'd rigged his bedroom with cameras and that he had everything, the whole night and the next morning. There must have been at least two because there were two distinct angles that were cut together in the video. The IT guy said it was pretty professional.'

'Oh, nice! Nothing like making you feel better about it, is there?' Zac frowned.

'Yes, that was a bit tactless. Generally speaking, I was interviewed by officers who were trained in dealing with this kind of crime and they were really good. James admitted his guilt soon after he was arrested, and so I was spared a court case.'

He nodded. 'But the video had already been shared.'

'Yes. The way that the group worked was that someone who wanted to join had to submit their own video, as a kind of entrance tariff. That meant that the group had a steady stream of new videos, and also that anyone who did join was immediately implicated so they couldn't betray any of the group's secrets.'

Zac shook his head, a look of utter disgust on his face. 'That's... I'd say it was clever if it wasn't so despicable.'

'It was effective, for quite some time. Not all of the members of the group worked at the hospital, and they still don't know exactly how many there were because when the first enquiries were made it shut down pretty quickly. Apparently most of the members were using burner phones, which didn't make things any easier.'

'And you didn't suspect anything?'

Allie shook her head. 'I just thought that we'd spent a nice night together, and that things hadn't worked out between us. I was hurt, but I got over it. But six months later, when someone blew the whistle on them, the hospital made all of the staff aware of what had happened and asked anyone who had concerns to come forward. And James suddenly wasn't at his desk. I put two and two together and...'

Suddenly it felt as if there wasn't enough air on the beach. Zac's hand hesitantly reached out for hers and she took it and gripped it tight, feeling the panic begin to subside.

'It's okay. I'm all right. Not too much more to go...'

'Take it at your own pace. I'll wait.'

He *would* wait. Even if this took all night. Allie took a breath, feeling stronger now.

'Some of the videos, mine included, had been posted on other closed groups and found their way out onto the internet. The police did what they could, and I did some research on how to find them. I got quite good at it, but as soon as I reported one and the task force got it taken down, another one would pop up.'

'You're still looking?'

Allie shook her head. 'No. It was driving me crazy, for a while it was all that I could think about and I'd be up all night searching. I had to let it go for the sake of my own sanity. Maybe we got everything and maybe we didn't. I've had to come to terms with that.'

Zac was shaking his head. 'How? How do you come to terms with something like this?'

'A lot of people helped me and…there wasn't much choice. These were things that I couldn't change and I had to learn to live with them.'

His fingers were gripping hers tightly now. 'Saying that I'm sorry this happened to you doesn't really cover it, Allie.'

'It's the best anyone can do. And I appreciate it.' She squeezed his hand, and felt his fingers relax against hers. 'Zac, I didn't tell you this to make you angry. I told you because I've decided I have to share this, and I want you to know first. If I can say it, then I feel a bit more in control of it.'

'Then thank you. For saying it.'

They sat for a while, hand in hand, watching the dark movement of the sea. Just existing, in an interval of time where it didn't seem necessary to do anything else.

'Australia does make a difference, doesn't it,' Allie murmured.

'It did to me. Maybe it's just the distance. If we were Australians we might be taking in a few galleries in London, or exploring the Roman ruins in St Albans. Finding our places there.'

'Maybe. It's a lot less cold here, though.'

'Yeah. Although winter in Sydney can go down to eight or nine degrees.'

'Oh. Freezing, then.'

Zac chuckled. 'It seems a bit colder, somehow. Australian houses are built for the heat so double glazing and central heating aren't so common here.'

'Or heavy curtains?' Allie nudged him. 'The price tag fell out of the curtains in my room this morning.'

'Did it?' Zac attempted an innocent look, shrugging when Allie raised her eyebrows. 'Okay. You've got me there. I didn't have any curtains in the bedroom, because it's not overlooked and I like the sea breeze at night. I thought you might appreciate a bit more privacy.'

'I did, very much. Along with the latch on the door and the new paint job.'

'Give me a break, eh? I'm not admitting to any of that, it could have happened for any reason and at any time. Just give me a few minutes and I'll come up with an alibi.'

Allie laughed. 'Better be a good one…'

He was laughing too, making a show of pretending to think. Out here together on the beach, it seemed so natural that they should be together, and so impossible that something this sweet could ever be happening to her. His fingers were twined around hers, and Allie knew that he felt it too. Zac would never act on it, and she'd never respond, but maybe the man who'd had to work so hard for that frank, open smile of his needed to hear it.

'I like you, Zac.'

The way he let go of her hand, the uncertainty on his face, showed that he knew exactly what she meant. But when he replied there was no trace that he understood the admission she'd just made. That she *wanted* him.

'I like you too, Allie.'

Maybe she should just leave it at that. Then she saw the pulse beating at one side of his brow.

'I meant… I *like* you. I know it's not going to come to anything, and that you'll be leaving soon. I just wanted you to know that it's the first time I've thought of anyone in that way for a long time.'

He smiled slowly, laying his hand on hers again. 'Is this all right, though?'

Holding hands? 'Yes, it's really nice.' Suddenly it felt as intimate as a kiss.

'And this?' He raised her hand, stopping when it was just a few inches from his lips.

Allie caught her breath. 'Yes.'

His lips brushed her fingers, his gaze holding hers in the most delicious of embraces. They both knew that this wasn't going anywhere, but somehow that made it all so much sweeter. There were no uncertainties, no doubts about what might happen next. Just the tender acknowledgement of what might have been, if their lives had been different.

'Look up.' He murmured the words, and Allie couldn't help but trust him and tilt her head towards the sky.

'Oh! Stars!'

'One thing you don't get in London. Too much light pollution. They're brighter still if you go a little further out of town.'

Zac brushed her fingers with his lips one more time, sending shivers up her spine. 'These are the stars I've been sleeping under for the last two years, though. So they're special to me.'

'Can we see the Southern Cross from here?' That was the only constellation from this hemisphere that Allie had heard of.

'Right there. You see, four stars in the shape of a cross.' He pointed towards the sky, just above the horizon, and Allie moved closer, leaning against his shoulder to see exactly where he was indicating. When his arm curled around her, she snuggled against him.

'It's smaller than I thought it would be. It's just those four?'

'There are more, but you need a good pair of binoculars or a telescope to see them.'

'Do you know any more?'

It was nice. Feeling the warmth of another human being. Someone who seemed to want to be here as much as she did. Feeling *Zac's* warmth.

'Do I know more? How long have you got…?'

Allie was alone now, with the curtains closed and her bedroom door latched. Which was crazy because the only other person in the apartment was Zac. But then the thoughts that had intruded now were crazy too. How James had seemed kind when she'd first met him. How she'd been so wrong once and it was difficult to trust her own judgement again.

But Zac was different. He'd been more than just honest with her, more than considerate. More than a friend in an unfamiliar place. He'd been someone who she could trust. Someone she might so easily have loved, if Allie hadn't found him too late for her to love anyone.

She lay down on the bed, switching out the light and then reaching to pull the covers up over her. In the velvet darkness, all she could think about was Zac's touch and the precious moments they'd spent together. Suddenly there was something very important that she had to do.

Stumbling to the door in the darkness, she quietly disengaged the latch. She might still need heavy curtains and closed windows, but tonight she could sleep without locking her bedroom door.

* * *

Last night had been the most exquisite experience...

Zac hadn't dated when he was a teenager. Taking a girl home was out of the question and anyway he was too busy with his studies, too desperate to get away from his mother's volatile moods and constant disapproval. When he'd got to university he'd diffidently embarked on relationships, usually with young women who were as shy as he was. In Australia, his growing confidence and his newfound love of the beach had widened his horizons a little, and he'd found himself with no shortage of offers, but even then his relationships had always been low-key. Always easy to make and easy to let go of. That childhood habit of never wanting anything that might be taken away had clearly controlled him more than he'd thought it did.

Allie was different, though. He'd felt a sizzling excitement from just a simple touch. He couldn't stop thinking about her, and when he managed to stop thinking and go to sleep he couldn't stop dreaming about her. Always wanting more, but knowing that whatever Allie could give him was somehow enough.

Thirty-two, and he was acting like a teenager. And Zac didn't care. Every moment he spent with Allie was confronting, exciting and more

. She waved to him and the effect was
, as if she were touching him.

 more thing to learn, in a world that al-
 seemed tipped on its head. Just the sight
, the knowledge that she might have been
ching him, was enough to set his heart rac-
. She walked to the edge of the balcony,
aning on the balustrade. Allie definitely *was*
watching him now.

He gave another wave, feeling a sudden, exquisite self-consciousness. That was new too.
Zac had always regarded his body as a means
to an end, something that allowed him to indulge in the activities that made him feel good.
But now all he could think about was whether
Allie liked what she saw.

All he wanted to do today was forget all of
the harms that the past had dealt them both.
Take the sunshine and the unpredictable swell
of the ocean, and see where that led. He jabbed
his finger towards the paddleboard that lay in
its bag on the empty beach, and gestured an invitation to Allie to join them. She nodded, disappearing off the balcony, leaving Zac to wait
for her on the beach.

On Monday morning Zac did his ward rounds
alone. He'd wished Allie good luck before she'd
gone to speak with Philippa, adding the caveat

fulfilling than he'd ever [...] plying a little logic to the si[...] self that it would never work [...] back off, wasn't an option any [...]

He'd woken early out of habit, [...] ically pulled on his board shorts. [...] out on the beach, testing out the wave [...] crashed across the ever-shifting sand.

'What's up with you, mate? That's an[...] one.' Mark hadn't failed to notice Zac's unforced errors.

'Work stuff.' Zac brushed off his lack of concentration in two words and Mark nodded, walking back out into the water and paddling out to the break.

Zac couldn't resist turning to look up at Allie's window. It was recessed slightly into the building, and screened by the plants and furniture on the deep balcony, but he could see the top of the sliding doors, and he couldn't help catching his breath. The curtains had been drawn back and the doors were slightly open.

Had she done the unthinkable, and allowed herself to sleep with the stars and the sea for company last night? Zac rejected the thought as too much to ask. But as he stared up at the balcony, unable to avert his gaze, he saw movement. Allie was up and dressed, and sitting that she didn't really need it, and she'd grinned nervously back at him.

'Thanks. I'll take the luck if you don't mind, all the same.'

Maybe he should have wished himself luck, he was nervous enough for both of them. Zac dismissed the thought and got on with his morning's work.

'What is it today, Jack?' When he'd entered the roomy four-person ward Zac had been under no illusions about what he'd find his next patient doing. And, true to form, he was playing computer games.

Jack ignored him, concentrating on the screen. He grinned suddenly, typing something and then looking up at Zac.

'Sorry, Dr Forbes.' Jack was nothing if not scrupulously polite. 'Just had to win this one.'

'In the interests of galactic peace and security?' Zac smiled.

'No, that's a different game. This one's Ancient Britain.'

'Right. Well, don't mess with the timeline, will you. I wouldn't want to disappear in a puff of smoke if you happen to vanquish one of my ancestors.'

Jack laughed. 'No chance of that, Dr Forbes. Unless you're descended from cosmic giants.'

'Ah. Should have known outer space would

be in there somewhere.' Zac laid the tablet he was carrying down on the bed, well out of Jack's reach. He'd already learned that it took Jack no time at all to call up his own notes and read them.

'Let's take a look at your leg, then.' Zac cleared the trailing cables and closed the laptop, putting it to one side on the cabinet next to the bed. 'Any chance of you going down to the rec room to play there?'

'I get interrupted.' Zac nodded, wordlessly noting that this was the whole point of going to the rec room. 'And this is more private, I'm playing with my girlfriend.'

'Right. Has she been in to see you?' Jack had plenty of visitors, but Zac didn't recall being introduced to a girlfriend.

'That's a bit difficult, she lives in Brisbane. I haven't met her yet IRL, but we're in a relationship.' Jack paused for a moment, frowning. 'IRL is In Real Life.'

'Gotcha.' Zac was already learning that a relationship didn't necessarily depend on the things he'd thought it did, and so he wasn't going to argue. He turned his attention to examining Jack's leg, which had been broken in several places in a car accident.

'The muscles are still wasted, Jack. How are the exercise sessions with your physio going?'

Jack shrugged. 'Okay.'

Zac knew exactly how they were going. Jack did all that was asked of him but no more. And when the session was over he returned to the empty ward and spent his time staring at the screen of his laptop instead of trying to walk as much as he could, as his physiotherapist had advised.

'Okay isn't good enough,' Zac reprimanded him gently. 'Before you leave here, we want to see you starting to do most of the things you usually can.'

'That's what I usually do…' Jack frowned, gesturing towards the laptop.

Zac pulled up a chair and sat down. One of the things he liked about working with teenagers and young adults was the challenge. And one of the things he'd learned was that directness and honesty was usually the best policy.

'Got tickets for the computer games conference in Melbourne next month?' Jack's mother had mentioned that to him, and Zac had stored the information away for future reference.

'Yes, I applied for them as soon as they went on sale…' Jack knew he'd fallen for the ruse, and frowned. 'I expect you're going to say that I'll be wanting to walk around there.'

'What do you think? I would have thought that having to rely on your parents pushing you around in a wheelchair would cramp your style a bit. Is your girlfriend going to be there?'

'Yes, I got her a ticket.'

'Take it from me. You're going to want to be on your feet when you meet her.'

Jack sighed, giving him a look that clearly indicated he thought Zac was around a hundred years old. 'Things are different from when you were young, Dr Forbes.'

'I like to think I'm still young enough to learn a thing or two. Enlighten me.'

'We don't care how someone looks. Everyone's the same inside.'

Excellent point. Jack had a lot going for him, he was intelligent, articulate and valued the people around him. But he was also fourteen, and Zac knew a bit more about life than he did.

'You fight with your girlfriend, do you?'

The question appeared to put Zac nearer to a hundred and fifty in Jack's eyes. 'I don't fight *with* her. We fight together, to vanquish oppression and injustice. We're comrades.'

Comrades was a good word. One that he might remember when talking with Allie. 'And, as comrades, you both have to be the best you can be, in order to face…whatever it is you're facing.'

'S'pose so… Yes, we have to keep our wits about us.'

'So here's the thing. If you truly couldn't make it back onto your feet, then you'd be right to expect that your girlfriend wouldn't see you any differently, and I'm glad that's something you both value and feel confident about in your relationship. But if you don't try, that's another thing entirely.'

Jack pursed his lips, thinking for a moment. 'You mean what's the point in being the best we can for each other online, if we can't do it IRL.'

'Couldn't have said it better myself.' Zac grinned at him. 'I know it's not easy to get back up and start moving around, but I wouldn't be pushing you if I didn't think you could do it.'

Jack frowned, clearly turning the idea over in his head. 'Yeah, okay. Chloe's a really good person and I'd like her to be proud of me. I'm really proud of the things she does.'

Jack gestured towards his laptop and Zac leaned back in his seat, not moving. The boy grinned at him and pulled himself across the bed, swinging his legs around. Zac helped him to stand, so that he could reach the laptop.

'Look, here…' Jack sank back onto the bed and tapped an address into the browser. 'This is Chloe's site.'

Zac stared at the screen. The website looked really professional, its message immediately clear, warning of the dangers of pollution and the erosion of the Australian coastline.

'How old is Chloe, Jack?'

The boy rolled his eyes. 'Don't worry. She's fourteen, same as me, we both know how to be careful online. We video-conference all the time, and my parents have met hers.'

'Right. Sorry. It's just that this looks amazing. Did she do it by herself?'

'No, I helped her. It's an important issue, and we both believe in preserving our natural resources. We don't just play games, you know.'

'Okay, I'm learning something.' Zac reached forward, tapping on a few of the menu links. The other pages were just as striking as the first. 'Is this kind of thing easy to do?'

'Where have you been, Dr Forbes?' Jack's voice held a note of resigned frustration. 'Don't you have to get stuff off the internet to be a doctor?'

'Yes, all the time. I don't have much to do with it apart from that.'

'Well, we're in the twenty-first century now. It's really easy to do something like this.'

Zac ignored the implied insult. 'Okay. Can I do you a deal? I'll share some of my knowledge with you, and we'll make a concerted effort to get you back on your feet. You share some of your knowledge with me, and show me how to make a website like that.'

'Cool. You're on.' Jack started to enter another web address into the browser and Zac stopped him.

'Not right now. First I'm going to take you through some of the exercises that your physiotherapist has given you to do in your own time, and we'll see how you do with them. Maybe we can meet up in the rec room, when I'm not on duty and you don't have any visitors, and you can impart some knowledge as regards web development.'

'The rec room.' Jack hadn't failed to notice that, and turned the corners of his mouth down in disapproval. 'Okay, whatever.'

Zac's head was buzzing with possibilities. Maybe Allie wasn't ready yet, but this was one way to take back something that had been taken from her. He'd have to test the water, but he couldn't even suggest it to her if he had no idea of how to accomplish it. He reached for Jack's walker, and put it by the side of the bed.

'This stays here, so you can reach it. Let's see you take a few steps. I want to see how much you can do…'

CHAPTER SEVEN

ALLIE HADN'T BEEN able to stop thinking about Zac lately. Surely he couldn't be unaware of the bonds that increasingly seemed to be pulling them together.

He'd been there for her this weekend and during her meeting with Philippa, as well. Not physically there, but she'd been able to explain what she wanted to do, despite the constant tug of anxiety that always accompanied talking about what had happened to her. Going through everything first with Zac hadn't just helped her arrange her thoughts effectively, it had given her the strength to speak out.

When she walked back onto the ward he was deep in conversation with the senior nurse, but he looked up and saw her as the doors closed behind her, flashing her a smile. He was clearly busy and when they found themselves alone for a moment she murmured that they'd talk later.

Later turned out to be lunchtime, when they

fetched sandwiches and a drink from the canteen and Zac guided her to a quiet place in the hospital grounds, where they could eat outside.

'How did it go?'

'Good. Great.' Allie was still slightly breathless from the feel of his light touch on her arm.

He nodded, clearly waiting for something a bit more tangible than that.

'Philippa suggested that we sit down together and talk about my experiences first. I agreed with her that it'll help us both move forward with a joint approach that might help Carly.'

He nodded. 'That sounds really sensible. How do you feel about it?'

'I'm really happy with it. It's practical and I feel supported in what I want to do. *More* supported, that is. I couldn't have done this without you, Zac.'

He pressed his lips together, looking a little disappointed. 'I'm glad I could help.'

Zac had his own set of insecurities about their relationship, and perhaps he thought that Allie needed him more than she wanted him. 'It's Philippa's job to help. You're my friend, and that's a bit different.'

He nodded. 'Philippa's very good. I'm sure she'll give you all of the professional support you need.'

'I've no doubt of it. I like her a lot.'

Something stirred in his eyes. Sweet shadows of a dark sea and glimmering stars. And there was an uncertainty in his face that matched her own. Allie supposed that was natural, when they were making their own rules and everything meant so much more than either of them were prepared to admit.

'You do? That's good.'

Allie leaned towards him. 'I *like* you a lot.'

Zac grinned suddenly. Job done. 'I *like* you a lot too. And I'm really glad that it went well for you this morning.'

Pure pleasure washed through her. It seemed they'd both needed a bit of reassurance.

There was still something on his mind, though. Zac was studying the ground in front of the bench where they were sitting as if it might be about to open up and swallow him.

'I was wondering. Since that's the case, how would you feel about coming on a date with me?'

A date? They were living in the same apartment, and Zac had already been eager to show Allie the best features of his adopted home.

She cleared her throat nervously. 'What kind of date, Zac?'

His face took on a pained expression and he seemed to be concentrating on fiddling with the wrapping of his sandwich. 'I was afraid you were going to ask that. You're quite right, we need to set a few boundaries…'

Silence. Zac was clearly struggling with this as much as she was. A sudden glimpse of the shy man who found it difficult to meet anyone's gaze reminded Allie that of course he found this difficult.

'Zac, I…' She searched for a way to phrase what she really wanted to say to him.

And then he said it for her. Suddenly his gaze met hers. 'I guess that the least I can do while asking someone out is to look at them.'

'Yes, it inspires confidence. Lets me know where you're coming from.'

He acknowledged the heavy hint with a smile. 'Well… I was talking with Jack this morning, about putting his laptop down and concentrating a bit more on his rehab.'

Allie couldn't see the connection, but she went with the flow, nodding him on.

'He was telling me that his generation makes their own rules, as if I was about a hundred years old. He's got a point, though, it is up to us to make the rules. I'd like to be a special friend to you, and I think that means finding out the things that we each want to give and accept.'

Allie stared at him, dumbstruck, for a moment. Zac's expression became pained and she had to give him a reply before he decided he'd said the wrong thing and he should forget all about the idea.

'Zac, I think that's one of the nicest things anyone's ever said to me.'

'Really?' He grinned suddenly. 'I'm not great at this, am I...?'

'Has anyone ever told you that a guy who doesn't rely on his looks when he asks a woman on a date, but thinks about what she might want from him, is a sure winner?'

'Uh...? No, I don't think so. Maybe they did and I was a bit too nervous to notice.'

'Then listen up, Zac. I'd really like to go on a date with you, and you don't need to say any of the right things to me, just tell me what you want. And, in case you're in any doubt, I'm not saying yes because I've been hurt, it's because I won't settle for anything less.'

That intoxicating warmth filtered into his gaze and Allie wondered for a moment what she *would* actually settle for. Right now it seemed a possibility that she might forget the hurt...

She could forget James. She could even trust Zac. But the shame and humiliation that had been heaped on her had changed Allie's relationship with her own body, making her conscious of it and uncomfortable with it. Zac had been willing to talk about anything in his life, and if being with him felt like having sex with a

...because *he* was the stranger.

...he stranger.

...change your mind?' His

...just getting used to the idea.' Holding...nds with him was nice. That was one ...ing she could take back right now, and she curled her fingers around his.

'Okay. How does Saturday evening sound?'

Allie smiled up at him. 'I think I'm free on Saturday evening. Did you have something in mind?'

'I thought I'd just weigh up the options for a while. Agonise a bit over them…' He gave her a cheery smile. 'Do you have any preferences?'

'I'd like…' in for a penny, in for a pound '…somewhere I can wear a dress.'

He nodded, smiling. 'A dress it is. I'm looking forward to it.'

In one way, Allie's obvious caution about their date made things a lot easier. Zac wasn't in the habit of steering his relationships the way he wanted them to go, and even if he'd aspired to do that he reckoned he didn't have the panache to get away with it. Allie was clearly unsure about how far she wanted to take this, and it was nice to be able to start a relationship with-

out any preconceptions. Nothing assume
ing taken for granted.

Zac's usual choice of venue for a summer
involved the open air—a barbecue maybe,
the beach. Somewhere that Allie could wear
dress was a little more of a challenge for him to
rise to. But he'd come up with an idea and some
last-minute tickets. The weekend had finally
arrived—anticipation making the journey a little slower than usual—and an hour before they
needed to leave the apartment, he'd changed
into a pale-coloured lightweight suit with an
open-necked shirt. Then he waited for Allie to
come back downstairs.

He wasn't aware of jumping to his feet when
he saw her, just that he was suddenly standing. Allie was wearing a plain dark blue sleeveless dress with high heels. Her hair was artfully
arranged so that her curls seemed softer and
wilder, and she wore make-up. The wrap that
covered her shoulders might be there for protection rather than warmth, but she'd clearly made
an effort.

'You look beautiful.' He wasn't sure where
they stood with regards to compliments yet, but
he allowed himself this one on the basis that it
was more understatement than compliment. She
shone, like moonlight over the sea.

And then she smiled, adding a whole new

dimension to his pleasure. 'Thank you. Not so bad yourself...'

She walked towards him and Zac's heart nearly stopped when she reached out, deftly pulling the collar of his shirt straight. Trying to catch his breath without seeming to, he held his arm out and she took it, letting him walk with her down to the car and open the passenger seat door for her.

Her eyes widened a little when he parked the car for their first stop. A food truck on the beach wasn't the obvious start to a date with a dress, but they had to eat.

'I couldn't get a dinner reservation for the restaurant at our final destination.' Zac felt a little flutter of excitement when Allie glared at him in frustration over the secret. 'So I reckoned that the best burger in town and the finest dining area imaginable would have to do.'

She looked at the wooden trestle tables set out on the beach. There were a few families, clearly relaxing after a hard day at the beach, and another couple who seemed on their way out for the evening.

'This is perfect, Zac. I love the décor.' She reached down, taking off her shoes and leaving them in the footwell.

Zac guided her to an empty seat and Allie sat with her back straight and her feet tucked under

her seat, looking like a queen. He fetched ham-
burgers and a fresh green salad to share, along
with plenty of napkins, and Allie ate with the
kind of appreciation that would generally be re-
served for a five-star restaurant. Then he hurried her back to the car, and started to drive
again.

He took a slightly longer route into Sydney,
taking in some of the best sightseeing loca-
tions of the city centre. By the time he parked
at Darling Harbour, Allie was looking around
her, drinking it all in.

'A ferry?' She was holding his arm, practically dragging him towards the pedestrian
walkway that led onto the craft.

'Best way to see the harbour...' Actually the
second best way. Their route home again, surrounded by the lights of the city, would be the
best way, but Zac wasn't going to give up even
that small detail of his plans for the evening.

Allie insisted on sitting on the open deck,
despite his warnings that they might encounter
some spray as the ferry began to move. It was
a twenty-minute ride to Circular Quay and she
hung onto his arm the whole way, craning her
neck to get the best views of the Harbour Bridge
and the Opera House. When Zac rose, guid-
ing her off the ferry, she seemed almost disap-

pointed, but then Allie turned her attention to the next thing on their agenda.

'We're going to see the Opera House?'

He nodded, loath to give away any more details. Zac led the way up the long series of steps, letting her stop every now and then to take everything in, and then into the building.

'A recital?' Allie was looking around her as they followed the path of the foyer, winding around the concert hall. 'You're a fan of the opera?'

Zac grinned. 'I've never been. It's about time I did, though, and even if it's not our thing then at least we can both say we've been to the Sydney Opera House.'

'Good thinking. How on earth did you get tickets at such short notice?'

'Beth helped, she's a real music buff and has a membership of the Opera House. She called the priority booking line for me and asked if there were any ticket returns.'

'That was nice of her.' Allie grinned up at him. 'Did you tell her who you were taking?'

Zac hadn't told anyone, not even Mark and Naomi. It had seemed somehow wrong to say even one word about this, when everyone back in London knew far too much about Allie's last relationship.

'I said I had a date with someone I wanted to

impress. Beth interrogated me a bit, and when I wouldn't give her a name she said that she was glad to see I was finally taking a more serious attitude to dating. So if you happen to mention it to her, I'd be grateful if you didn't say that we ate on the beach.'

Allie's sudden shiver and the warmth in her face reminded him again just how wounded she was. When she moved a little closer to him, as if she'd just gained more confidence in his protection, Zac thanked his lucky stars that he'd been careful.

'Not a word about the beach, I promise. Although it did seem quite in keeping with the occasion, since we didn't get our feet wet.'

Zac laughed, and she squeezed his arm. This was already shaping up to be the best date he'd ever been on. A redefinition of the word *date* in fact...

They had great seats, and the music... Zac knew nothing about music, and wasn't accustomed to sitting quietly in an auditorium, but the music had a texture all of its own. Swelling and then receding, like the ocean. Washing over them in the darkness, an almost physical pleasure that made him shiver at times. Allie seemed to feel it too, forgetting to adjust the wrap when it slipped from her shoulders. If he chose to see it that way, Zac could imagine her beginning to let down her guard and letting the music in to sit beside her. He could almost feel jealous of it, but he knew that this was precious. If the music could reach Allie, then so could he.

'What did you think?' As they walked back down the steps of the Opera House, Zac asked the question.

'I loved it. Thank you.' Allie pulled her wrap back around her shoulders, but since most of the other women he could see were donning jackets, Zac decided not to take it personally. Although maybe he could take the shining look on Allie's face a little personally.

They turned to see the projections that now caressed the sails of the Opera House. And then he hurried her back down to the terminus to catch the next ferry.

'It's wonderful! Sydney's such a beautiful city.' Allie had again decided that only the deck of the ferry would do, and she was shivering slightly in the cool breeze. Zac took off his jacket, deciding that it was possible to worry too much about how everything he did might seem, and offered it to her.

'Thanks. Aren't you chilly now?'

He chuckled. 'Yeah. Don't give it back, whatever you do.'

She laughed, pulling his jacket around her

gratefully. 'I've really enjoyed this evening, Zac. It feels…like a taste of the life I used to have.'

'That's good?' Zac wondered whether Allie had really thought that through.

'I just…' Allie leaned against the handrail, looking down at the water. 'I just want to go back to the way things were. The way *I* used to be.'

She seemed to be asking him something. Zac could hardly bear the answer that he knew he had to give, because anything else was wishful thinking at best. At worst, a bare-faced lie.

'You can't go back, Allie. I wish that were possible, but none of us can, we can only go forward. And you never know, forward might be better than back.'

She looked up at him, seeming to be blinking away tears. 'Thank you. I've been telling myself that over and over again and… It's nice when someone else is honest enough to say it.'

Allie pressed her lips together, looking round. The ferry was nearing the dock and the impetus to go forward seemed to seize her once more. 'It's time to go.'

'Not yet. Allie, listen…' She must have heard the urgency in his voice because she turned, looking back at him.

'I don't know how I'd cope with the kind of abuse that you've been subjected to. I have no idea how you're going to cope with it either. But I believe that you will. Things won't be the same, but you'll find your own peace and make a life that you can care about.'

'You *believe?*' She threw the question at him, as if it were a challenge.

'If you don't, what are you doing here with me? It's far less trouble to sit at home...'

The hurt must have sounded in his voice, because Allie's face suddenly softened. She reached out, slipping her hand around his elbow, and Zac automatically crooked his arm.

'I'm here because I want to be. With you.'

That was suddenly enough. More than just enough. It was everything. Zac laid his hand on hers, feeling her fingers squeeze his arm.

He made another detour on the way home, to take in the lights of Sydney, glinting across the water of the bay. Allie held his hand as they climbed the steps back up to the apartment, stopping outside the door.

'The Opera House was wonderful. Thank you, Zac.'

'Thank *you*. I have a great memory to take back to London with me.'

Allie laughed. 'I can't believe you've been here all this time and you hadn't been there.'

She didn't seem about to move, and Zac felt

in his pocket for his key to the apartment. Suddenly Allie reached up, smoothing the lapel of his jacket. A brief, intoxicating trace of her scent made him stop in his tracks, and when he looked down at her Allie's gaze met his.

First date. Doorstep. He was getting the message. Zac just didn't quite know how to respond to it. Then it occurred to him that he should just ask, because Allie was perfectly capable of saying no.

'Could we do this again?'

'I'd love to. Only next time I'd like it to be my surprise. Are you free next weekend?'

Zac thought the matter over. He might know the area better than she did, but where they went really wasn't the point. He just wanted to go there with Allie.

'Nothing planned. Any time next weekend sounds perfect.'

He probably should open the door now. Maybe make some hot chocolate to round the evening off, in the hope that would put him in the mood for sleep because right now it felt as if every one of his senses was on high alert. He could feel the movement of the breeze, hear the crash of the sea behind them. And all he could see was Allie...

'May I...' He lost his nerve and then she stepped a little closer. 'May I kiss you?'

'I'd like that, very much.'

He caught her hand, raising her fingers to his lips. Each sensation seemed magnified, dizzying. Then Zac brushed his lips against her cheek. Allie moved a little closer still, resting her hand on his shoulder, and he bent to kiss her mouth.

As kisses went, it wasn't the longest or the most passionate. But it was intoxicating, in a way that he'd never experienced before. This slow, make-your-own-rules way of doing everything made everything more uncertain, but a hundred times more pleasurable. Each time they touched he knew for sure that it was because Allie wanted to touch him, enough to cross the line that she'd drawn around herself.

'That was gorgeous. Perhaps we should go in now.' He felt her breath against his neck, and shivered at its caress.

'I could…see you inside and then go back to the car. You could watch me from the window.' He teased her and Allie laughed.

'Where are you going to go? You live here!'

'I'd just drive for a while and then sneak in. I'll be quiet, in case you're asleep.'

'You think I could sleep, when I'd be wondering if I'll hear you creeping up the stairs at any moment? And if I didn't hear you, then I'd have to go out and look for you in case you'd had an accident. That's not a good ending to the evening, is it, Zac?'

'Probably not.' Zac decided to revert to the original plan. 'Hot chocolate then?'

'That would be nice.' She took the key from his hand, and opened the door.

Allie perched herself on one of the breakfast bar stools, slipping her shoes off and watching him as he prepared the hot chocolate. Zac could almost feel her gaze, and concentrated on steadying his hands so he didn't burn himself. When he slid a full mug across to her she picked it up and took a taste.

'Mmm. That's really nice, thank you. I'm going to take it upstairs if that's okay?'

'Of course. Sleep well.'

'You too. And thank you again for a lovely evening...'

Zac watched as she bent to pick up her shoes. She blew a kiss which seemed to hit his temple with a dizzying blow, then made for the stairs. He listened for the sound of her footsteps and when he heard her bedroom door open and then close, he slid back the doors that opened onto the balcony.

If he had a *thinking place* then this was probably it. Somehow, the regular crash of the sea and the light from the stars always put everything into its proper focus. But that process wasn't going to work this time, because the correct perspective was that everything Allie said and did mattered a lot more than it should to him.

He was leaving. Allie was… Zac thought for a moment and discounted the word *fragile,* along with *vulnerable.* Allie was neither, but she'd been hurt so badly that it took considerable strength for her just to function, let alone come to a new country and start again. He'd thought that a low-key relationship, more friends than anything else, might be the right way to deal with the instant chemistry between them. It would allow them to acknowledge what was indisputably there, without either of them getting too involved. And that might well have worked if their relationship *was* low-key.

But when they talked there was an honesty that made Zac feel exposed, naked almost. When they touched it set off a chain reaction of pleasure that shot through him with such force that it left him breathless.

He couldn't go back, not now, even if there was the ever-present fear of losing something he cared about. As long as Allie wanted to be with him, he'd be there for her. If it broke his heart to leave, then so be it.

Allie had carefully measured her own footsteps as she climbed the stairs. Made sure she didn't run to her room and bang the door closed behind her. She closed the curtains, flipped on the light and then sat down on the bed.

She'd wanted all of this. Wanted to feel something again, and more than anything she'd wanted to feel it with Zac. And she'd loved everything about the evening and the way he'd planned it so carefully.

He was going back to London and she would be staying here in Sydney. But that didn't make any difference. She felt what she felt, and the shy side of Zac's nature gave her the courage to show it. This was the slow reawakening that she'd longed for, and which was so sweet it almost hurt. Like pale winter skin that was exposed to the sun for the first long hot day of summer and felt tender afterwards.

Allie put the hot chocolate down beside the bed and changed into her nightdress, adding her dressing gown on top of it, even if it was a little too warm for comfort. She was bound to feel a little uncertain about this. All that Allie really knew was that she finally felt she had a choice about what she was going to do next, and that she chose not to give Zac up until the time came for him to leave.

CHAPTER EIGHT

Work had been Allie's way of surviving over the last eighteen months. She'd piled everything into it, as a way of shutting out the thoughts that tormented her, but now she was beginning to realise that she'd forgotten something. Having a life outside the hospital made her sharper and better during the hours she spent working.

She and Zac stared at the empty bed, the pillows still showing the indentation of a head. The leads from the intravenous drips were draped along the floor, along with a few spots of blood where their patient had pulled the catheter from the back of her hand. Corinne had been brought into the ward this morning from the ED, suffering from a kidney infection and sepsis, and she'd been started on broad spectrum antibiotics and fluids immediately. By the time she'd reached the ward all of the necessary tests to check that her other organs hadn't been compromised had been completed, and Allie and

Zac had reviewed her condition and medication, then left her to rest. And now, two hours later, she was gone.

'I've only been away five minutes...' The nurse who was attending her had re-entered the room behind them.

'You were monitoring her condition regularly,' Zac murmured, reassuring the nurse. 'We need to put the search procedure in place though. Will you go and speak with the ward manager, please.'

The nurse hurried away, and Zac shot Allie a worried look. Corinne's condition had been caught early and, although sepsis was always a cause for concern, she was stable and hadn't displayed any of the confusion that was one of the possible symptoms.

'What's the procedure, Zac?'

'The doctor on shift for a missing patient checks their room, and reports back to the ward manager. You'll look through her personal items?'

Allie nodded, opening the closet. There was precious little in it, just a crumpled T-shirt, a bra and a folded newspaper. 'Nothing here, she's probably wearing her clothes on top of her hospital gown. I remember the nurse putting them in here for her, there was a red hoodie. And I got her to let go of her handbag and put it in here, it was one of those leather courier bags.'

Zac nodded, taking the pillows from the bed and pulling the covers back to check beneath them. 'Nothing here to give us a clue. There are some spots of blood on the floor, and a smudge on the towel dispenser so her hand's probably bleeding from where she pulled the IV out. It doesn't look as if she's touched anything else.'

They made their way to the ward manager's office, reporting back to her.

'Thanks. Let's hope she's wearing the hoodie, eh, she'll stand out a bit in that. Can you go and do Sector Six now?' She handed Zac a sheet of paper from the file that was already open on her desk, and Allie saw a plan of the ward with different sectors outlined in red, and a checklist.

'Right you are. Thanks.'

Allie followed him to the rec room, and then on to the kitchen next door. They methodically checked everything for any signs that Corinne had been this way, ticking items from the checklist as they went. When they returned to the ward manager's office she was already on the phone.

'I've got the last sector check complete now.' She took the sheet of paper back from Zac. 'We're sure she's not still on the ward… Yes, okay… Thanks.'

'No sign of her?' Zac pressed his lips together in disappointment.

'No. There's quite a large smudge of blood on the wall next to the door release button, which can't have been there for long, so we think she's left the ward. We checked outside in the corridor and there's nothing there to show which way she went. All of the other wards in this block are doing a missing patient check, and we already have security on all of the possible exits and the walkway through to the main building.'

'So the common area search will be starting now?' Zac asked.

The ward manager nodded. 'Yes. It might take a while, but they'll find her.'

Allie puffed out a breath as they walked out of the office. 'I dare say there are as many places to hide in this hospital as there are at the one back home in London.'

Zac nodded. 'More, possibly. The footprint's bigger so there's a bit more space. She may not be hiding.'

'She's in a strange place and we know she isn't thinking straight, because if she was she wouldn't have pulled out her IVs. I reckon we'd better hope she's hiding, because otherwise she's managed to slip past security.'

'That doesn't bear thinking about. She could be anywhere.'

'I reckon she would have gone home.' The idea started to take hold in Allie's head and she suddenly couldn't let it go. 'It's unlikely but…'

Zac nodded. '*Highly* unlikely. We missed her pretty quickly and she would have had to move quickly to slip past security before we raised the alarm.'

'Coming to the wrong conclusions doesn't make someone any less determined. Confusion and thinking that you're going to die are both symptoms of sepsis, and patients have been known to try to walk out of hospitals before. Where else do you go when you're feeling awful?'

'There's not much more we can do here, other than search places we've already searched.' Zac marched back to Corinne's room, picking up the tablet that contained all of their patients' notes for the morning and tapping it. 'We have her address and it's not far.'

He was suddenly on the move again, hurrying back to the small bank of lockers in the staff kitchen and retrieving his car keys. Her instinct and his capacity for action carried them into the ward manager's office and then through security and into the car park.

'This is the street.' They'd driven for ten minutes. 'Can you look out for the numbers?'

Small one-storey properties, set back from

the road. Allie scanned them, trying to see house numbers, and then she didn't need to. Up ahead, a taxi had drawn up and she saw a flash of red as a slight figure got out of the back seat.

'There, Zac!'

He put his foot down, accelerating up the road. As they went past the taxi the driver wound down his window, leaning out.

'Hey! Miss…!'

Corinne had clearly been so focused on getting to her front door that she'd forgotten to pay, and she didn't look round. Zac stopped beside the taxi, pulling his wallet from his pocket.

'What's the damage, mate?'

Allie kept going, running to head Corinne off. She caught up with her halfway up the path, seeing Zac pull out his phone as the taxi drew away and speaking quickly into it, clearly calling to let the ward manager know that she could call off the search now. He waited at the end of the path, keeping his distance so that he didn't spook Corinne.

'Hey, Corinne. How are you doing?' Allie slowed down, smiling at her. Corinne had a paper towel wrapped around her hand, and her hospital gown was tucked into her jeans, showing only at the neck of her hoodie.

'Okay…' She clearly wasn't okay but she kept

walking, probably more out of muscle memory than anything else.

'Corinne, stop.' Allie blocked her path, and Corinne stared blankly at her. 'You know who I am—Allie, the doctor from the hospital.'

Recognition showed in Corinne's eyes. 'I'm… I need to go inside now. I'll be okay.'

Allie addressed the balance between telling Corinne that she definitely wouldn't be okay if she didn't come back to the hospital, and frightening her with that information.

'If you come back to the hospital with us, you'll be okay. If you stay here, you won't.'

'If I'm going to die, I'd rather do it at home. Thanks for all the trouble you've taken, but you don't need to worry any more.' Corinne's face was impassive, which was what worried Allie the most. The feeling of dying was a symptom of sepsis, and Corinne seemed to have accepted that this was what was going to happen.

'Listen to me, Corinne. I'm a doctor…' Allie knew she had to give Corinne a clear way forward right now. 'It's not unusual for people to feel the way you do right now, but you need to come back to the hospital with me. If you do, I promise you that I can get you better and you won't die.'

Rash promises, based on probabilities rather than all the things that could possibly happen in real life. But Allie recognised the annoyed look that Corinne shot in her direction. There was a measure of peace in accepting that things couldn't get better, and when others—most notably Zac—had changed her own view of life, it had hit Allie hard.

'I've been so much trouble…' A tear rolled down Corinne's face.

'That's what I get paid for, taking trouble. Without any patients I'd be out of a job.' Allie took her arm, firmly starting to walk her back along the front path.

'I don't know. I feel bad. Maybe I should just stay here and lie down for a while…' Corinne started to protest and Allie ignored her, keeping her walking.

'Let me decide what's best. I've got you, Corinne, and you'll be safe with me, I promise.'

Corinne didn't reply but she didn't stop walking. Allie decided to take that as an agreement for treatment, but as Corinne's blind focus on getting home seemed to dissipate, her legs began to buckle. Allie tried to hold her up, but Zac was there, lifting Corinne up in his arms and carrying her towards the car.

Allie fished his car keys from his pocket, trying not to think about the intimacy involved in the necessary gesture. She opened the back door, pushing a bag full of surfing equipment to one side, and Zac deposited Corinne gently on the seat, pulling the seat belt across her. Allie put his car keys into his hand and got in next to Corinne, putting her arm around her to reassure her. Zac got into the driver's seat, performing a U-turn in the road, and Allie allowed herself to breathe a sigh of relief.

A nurse was waiting at the edge of the car park with a wheelchair, and Zac drew up next to her. They walked briskly past the security officer at the main door and took Corinne back up to the ward. She was gently undressed and put back to bed, and Allie turned her attention to re-inserting the catheter and starting up the lifesaving drips again.

'Doesn't look too bad.' Zac had clipped a blood pressure and heart rate sensor to Corinne's finger and was looking at the screen by the side of the bed. 'Will you stay and check her over more thoroughly?'

'Yes, and I'll take a look at where she pulled the catheter out.' Blood was soaking through the paper towel that was wrapped around Corinne's hand. 'I'd like to sit with her for a while as well.'

Zac nodded. 'Good idea. I can get on and finish the rounds.'

Corinne was curled up in the bed, her eyes closed, and Allie suspected that she was zoning out rather than sleeping. That was fine, but it would be good to be able to talk with her a little and reassure her. When the antibiotics started to take effect she should start to feel much better and would be more receptive.

Zac made his way to the door, and she felt a sudden sense of loss. Allie swallowed it down, turning to Corinne.

'Good call, by the way.' Zac had turned and was smiling at her, and suddenly Allie's world turned from shadow into sunshine.

'You too.' She smiled back at him. Zac's approbation shouldn't be important, they'd taken a chance that might have been wrong but had turned out to be right. But he'd trusted her judgement, weighed the matter up and decided it was worth a try. That meant more than it should.

Allie had stayed with Corinne for two hours, and then popped back during the afternoon to check on her, while Zac busied himself with all of the other things on their schedule. That was the advantage of having two doctors doing one person's job for a few weeks, but Zac was pleased it had worked out that way. Her own battle to find peace seemed to have deepened and broadened the already good relationship Allie created with her patients.

'We'll pop in to see Corinne before we go?' As they wrapped up their shift Zac knew that

Allie would ask, and reckoned he might as well save her the trouble.

They found her sitting up in bed with a half-eaten plate of food in front of her. Zac motioned to the nurse who was taking her blood pressure that it would be okay to leave them here with Corinne for a while.

'Hey! You've managed to eat something.' Allie's smile showed that she wasn't going to bother about the half of the plate that was full and was concentrating on the half that was empty.

'Yeah, I was hungry, I hadn't eaten in a while. I wasn't well for a few days before I called for help.' Corinne gave her an embarrassed smile. 'I'm really sorry. About earlier...'

Allie plumped herself down on the chair next to Corinne's bed. 'I'm just happy to see you looking so much better. And there's something I want to say to you.'

Corinne turned the corners of her mouth down, obviously expecting a telling-off. Zac begged to differ. Whatever it was that Allie had to say, she wouldn't be reproving Corinne. He decided that she didn't need him to help her and sat down on a chair in the corner.

'One of the symptoms of sepsis is that people tend to do things they wouldn't normally do. That's really well understood. So I don't want you to apologise or beat yourself up over it. It's like saying sorry for not being able to walk when you've broken your leg.'

Corinne nodded, still looking unconvinced.

'What is it, Corinne?' Allie sat back and waited.

'Did I…? I did, didn't I? I said that if I was going to die, then I wanted to do it at home. That was really stupid.'

'No, it's not. Feeling as if you're dying is a recognised symptom of sepsis and in these situations instinct takes over and your first priority is to be somewhere that's familiar. Not many people get as far as you did, but I guess that just means you're a bit more resourceful than most.'

Corinne stared at her, wide-eyed. 'You're just saying that, aren't you?'

Allie turned to Zac, indicating that it was time for him to back her up on this. 'No, Allie's not just saying it. Ask any ambulance crew, they've all had to persuade people with very serious injuries that they won't be okay to go home if they're allowed to just rest for a minute.'

Corinne nodded. 'Thanks. I appreciate that.'

'Glad you're taking his word for it over mine…' Allie grinned, raising an eyebrow.

Corinne's hand flew to her mouth and then suddenly she started to laugh. Allie's teasing had done its job and taken the tension out of the situation. 'There's no right answer to that, is there?'

Zac chuckled. 'None that won't get you into trouble. I'd keep quiet if I were you.'

'Sounds like good advice.' Allie shot Zac a grin. 'Do you have someone who can bring you in some things?'

'Yes, thanks. My parents are in Melbourne, but my brother and sister-in-law will be coming this evening. With some clothes and probably a set of shackles in case the nursing staff need them.' Corinne was able to venture a joke about it now.

'They won't. You're looking much better now, and all of your charts tell me that you're on the mend.' Allie pursed her lips. 'Would you like me to speak to your brother, and tell him what I've told you?'

Corinne nodded. 'He won't be here for another hour or so but… I don't suppose you could phone him, could you? If it's not too much trouble.'

'Of course, that's no trouble at all. Give me his number…'

Allie spent some time with Corinne's brother on the phone, but she smilingly reported back that everything was fine, and that her brother understood. Corinne seemed a great deal happier now, and Allie bade her a cheerful farewell.

'What are the arrangements here with regards to Post Sepsis Syndrome?' Allie asked as they walked down to the car together.

'There's an information pack, and we usually have a session with patients or caregivers, to go through it with them and chat about any specific concerns they have. They have a number they can call for help after they're discharged.' The emotional and physical after-effects of sepsis were well recognised now.

'That's good, thanks. Can I have a copy of the pack to look through it?'

'I'll get you one tomorrow. I think you've made a good start in allaying Corinne's fears though. I didn't hear her say that she'd gone home because she was sure she was going to die.'

Allie nodded. 'She was so unemotional about it, as if she'd accepted that was going to happen and was acting accordingly. When she stumbled, I knew I'd got through to her...'

'That you'd persuaded her there was an alternative?'

'Yes. When she realised that, she lost her focus and almost fell.' Allie pressed her lips together, clearly deep in thought. 'It must have been hard for her. Suddenly realising that she had something to lose.'

Zac nodded. It must have been hard, but he

got the impression that Allie wasn't talking only about Corinne. 'Better than not allowing yourself anything, in case you lose it.'

'Really?'

He nodded. 'Yes. Really.'

She smiled up at him suddenly. 'Are you still up for letting me drive us home this evening?'

'Absolutely.' He took his car keys from his pocket and dropped them into her hand. 'Or you could just tell me where we're going at the weekend, so that I can drive. I may be able to suggest a better route.'

Allie chuckled. 'Nice try, Zac. You're not convincing me. I can read a map.'

Zac shrugged. They were both beginning to focus on the delicious possibilities of the present instead of the past, and there was always a possibility that either he or Allie might stumble. But, for now, they were both keeping their footing.

He got into the car and Allie started the engine, driving confidently out of the car park.

CHAPTER NINE

Allie had driven to and from the hospital a few times now, with Zac sitting next to her in the passenger seat. Driving a car as large as Zac's was unfamiliar, and she kept forgetting that it had an automatic transmission and reaching for the gear stick. But after a bit of practice, and a careful read-through of the Australian Road Rules, she was confident she could make the longer drive in the dark that she had in mind for their date on Friday evening.

He'd complied without question when she'd told him to bring a sweater with him, although Allie could see that he had his doubts about whether that was absolutely necessary. And she'd been through the large closet in the apartment's entrance lobby, moving the mountain of surfing gear out of the way to find a warm jacket with gloves in the pockets at the back. Allie had surreptitiously added that to her own jacket in the boot of the car. They were ready to go, and Allie switched on the satnav, calling up the route she'd programmed in.

After they'd been driving for a while, heading away from the centre of Sydney, Zac began to get a little restive.

'We're not lost, are we?' He was staring out at the high bushes that bordered the highway.

'No.' She grinned at him. 'I'm not, anyway.'

'Okay. I'll just go with the flow, shall I? Unless you have any navigational questions you want to ask…'

'Like, how do I get to where we're going?'

He chuckled. 'Yeah. That would be ideal.'

'I've held out this long and I'm not going to give it away now. I have an innate sense of direction and a satnav.' And Allie was increasingly nervous. What if Zac didn't enjoy the evening she'd planned? What if it gave too much away about her feelings for him and he was embarrassed by them?

It wasn't long before they entered the Royal National Park, which gave their destination away, but Zac still seemed mystified, obviously wondering what they'd be doing here when it would be getting dark in less than an hour. But as they climbed towards higher ground he started to grin, and when Allie turned off the road and he caught sight of the observatory platform he chuckled.

'Stargazing?'

'Yes, I hope you'll like it.'

'It's a great idea, Allie. Thank you.' He got out of the car, looking around to get his bearings. 'I haven't heard of an observation point in this area.'

'It's new, they've just opened up this year apparently. When I compared the various websites it seemed to be good, and it has the advantage of being close to Sydney. This is why we had to come on a Friday, all of the tickets for Saturday were already gone.'

He nodded, looking around. The advertised telescope looked reassuringly large and complicated, and there was a man standing next to it chatting to a few of the other people who were here for the evening. The breeze was already cooler at this height, and Zac shrugged off a shiver.

'I've brought our coats.' She opened the boot of the car, handing him his, and he grinned, pulling it on.

'Thanks. When you said dress warmly, I didn't think I'd need any more than a sweater.'

She led him over to the small kiosk that was serving thick soup and submarine rolls and they ate hungrily. The light was fading fast and the first few stars were beginning to appear in the sky, and they joined the other stargazers in a group around the telescope as the astronomer began to explain which star was which and what they'd be doing this evening. High-powered binoculars were available for everyone, and they would all have their turn with the telescope.

But just her own eyes and the scattering of bright stars that were appearing in the sky were enough to make Allie catch her breath. She nudged Zac, whose attention seemed taken up by the telescope. 'I saw pictures of this on the web. I thought they were enhanced in some way.' She grinned up at him.

'No, this is what it's really like. You can capture it with a photograph, but it doesn't really do it justice, does it?'

Photographs lied. Even when they weren't enhanced or changed in any way, the lens could only capture one moment that didn't take any notice of the human heart… Allie rejected the thought, and her own shiver of humiliation.

'It's amazing.' Something that was an unchangeable force of nature. 'Have you been stargazing before?'

'I've seen the stars from the park before, but never with a telescope or anyone to explain it all.' His gaze settled back eagerly onto the telescope. 'I can't wait for our turn…'

The time was spent chatting with the others in the small group, swapping stories and impressions. Allie found that the binoculars allowed her to see the craters of the moon, and the long sweep of the Milky Way. The clarity of the universe around her made her catch her breath.

'It makes you feel as if you're a part of it all, doesn't it?'

Zac chuckled. 'Yes, I'm feeling like an extremely small part of it all at the moment. It puts everything into perspective.'

Passing unnoticed, under the great panorama of the sky. It was a great feeling. Allie snuggled against Zac and he put his arm around her shoulders. *That* was a great feeling too.

The first hour was taken up with images from the telescope, displayed on a screen so that everyone could see them. There was something about stars that made everyone move just a little closer together.

Then came their chance to direct the telescope wherever they wanted in the night sky. Zac was so transfixed by it all, so excited, but he didn't forget to give Allie her turn and she saw a bright nebula, swirling slowly but unstoppably in a blaze of colour. Far distant stars, the images of which were hundreds of years old after having travelled at the speed of light through the universe. The moon, their closest neighbour, was revealed in intricate detail which made Allie almost feel that she could reach out and touch it.

It all lasted for longer than had been advertised, and the young woman who was dispensing more soup from the kiosk told Allie laughingly that it always did.

'We give a time, but we never expect to stick to it. People always want to stay a bit longer. Between you and me, *I* always want to stay a bit longer, the sky's different every night.'

'So you never get bored with your job?'

'How could I? Would you like me to take a photograph of you?'

Allie hesitated. She'd seen several people standing in front of the camera that was mounted on a tripod to one side of the kiosk, and decided not to join in with that part of the evening.

'I'm not really...very photogenic.'

The woman raised one eyebrow, but clearly decided not to make a point of it. That was good. Most people allowed Allie to melt away quietly when photographs were being taken, but there was always someone who insisted she move a little closer to be included in the shot.

'The camera's adjusted to capture the stars. Anything on the ground comes out as just a silhouette.'

Allie thought about the idea, beginning to like it. 'Okay. If you don't mind.'

There was no one else waiting for soup, and the woman climbed down from behind the counter in the kiosk. Allie chose the section of the night sky that she wanted the photograph to capture, and suddenly Zac was there, standing beside her, wanting to know what was going on.

'We're taking a photo…' Allie couldn't help feeling slightly apologetic as she looked up at him, as if this was some kind of guilty secret.

'Ah. With an anonymous shadow beneath it?' Zac got the point almost immediately.

'Yes. Don't you feel a bit like an anonymous shadow at the moment?'

He chuckled. 'A lot like one. This is all too big for us to be anything else, isn't it?'

'Both of you?' The woman had finished fiddling with the camera and was looking up at them now.

'Yes. Both of us.' Being a shadow didn't seem quite so melancholy if Zac was going to join her. 'Where do we stand?'

It was late when everyone said their goodbyes, and they got back into the car. Allie followed the line of headlights moving slowly along the road that led off the mountain, trying to concentrate in the darkness. Zac was in the passenger seat, flipping through the photographs that had been downloaded from the telescope onto his phone.

'You want me to drive?' He looked up suddenly as Allie slowed, confused by the shadows that formed around the edge of the beam of the headlights.

'Uh… Maybe.' She brought the vehicle to a stop, still hanging onto the steering wheel. 'I'm not used to this.'

'I should have remembered. Finding yourself in complete darkness comes as a bit of a shock after London.' He grinned, reaching to open the passenger door, and Allie remembered just in time to disengage the locks.

Stupid. Whenever she drove alone these days, she locked the car doors. But there was nothing out here… Nothing but shadows that suddenly seemed menacing. And creatures that she'd heard about but hadn't yet seen.

As Zac walked around to her side of the car she saw something move in the furthest reaches of the headlights. What seemed like a pair of eyes, reflecting the light, and then disappearing back into the shadows of the trees around them. And she panicked…

Allie knew exactly what was happening to her. These attacks had become frighteningly familiar when she'd first learned about what James had done, but she'd thought she had them under control. But in this unfamiliar darkness, surrounded by goodness only knew what…

She tried to breathe. Tried to let go of the steering wheel, but she couldn't, because that was the one thing that seemed to afford her a measure of control. She was aware of Zac opening the driver's door beside her, and couldn't help letting out a whimper of panic.

What must he think? That only made things worse, and she felt tears roll silently down her cheeks.

'Allie?' She heard Zac's voice beside her. Beckoning her back into the real world, where she could cope with the everyday things that surrounded her, but it wasn't enough. He closed the car door, walking back round to get into the passenger seat.

'You're okay. Breathe.'

That was what she was trying to do. Allie closed her eyes, trying to dispel the image of the scene around her. Darkness. Unknown things that seemed to be moving around in that darkness. It suddenly felt even more terrifying and she opened her eyes again, blinking into the pool of light around them. Searching...

Zac leaned forward slowly, engaging the locks on the car doors. She tried to focus on him, but shame wouldn't allow her to meet his gaze.

'Allie, listen. You're okay, you're safe. Just breathe with me.' His voice held no trace of reproach, just gentle reassurance. This time she *could* follow his lead, and as he counted slowly she managed to regulate the panicky gasps of air. Her head began to stop swimming.

'That's great. Now let go of the steering wheel before you break it in half.' His quiet humour cut into the panic, and Allie focused on her hands, willing her fingers to unclench.

'Good. Give it another try, you're nearly there.'

It was an effort, but she managed to let go, in favour of clasping her hands tightly together in her lap. 'Zac… I'm so sorry…'

'Don't be. You're on new territory and you're allowed to be uncertain. I should have thought about it sooner.'

Allie shook her head. 'I've spoiled everything…'

'No, you haven't. Get your phone out.'

Allie felt miserably in her pocket, pulling her phone out with trembling fingers.

'Let's take a look at that picture, eh?'

It was easy enough to find, it was the only image on her phone. Allie tapped on the screen and the picture of the stars, with two unrecognisable silhouettes beneath them, opened up.

'It's…' She cleared the lump that had formed in her throat. 'It's a great picture.'

'It was a wonderful moment. Thank you for sharing it with me.'

'You want me to send it to you?' The thought made her feel a little breathless, even if there was nothing to worry about.

He shook his head. 'No, I don't think so. I prefer having it up here.' Zac gave a diffident shrug, tapping his temple with one finger.

'I really *am* sorry, Zac. I was making a fuss over nothing.' She reached over, taking his hand. Zac hadn't touched her once, and his instincts had been good. If he had, it would only have made her panic even more.

'It's not nothing, Allie. It's something you've had to go through and I wish that you hadn't. But it doesn't change anything, about you or me.' He frowned suddenly. 'Am I explaining this properly?'

'You mean it's something that happens to me, not who I am?' Allie hoped that was what he was thinking, anyway.

'Yes, exactly.' He squeezed her hand. 'This is who *I* want to be.'

'Me too.'

Zac grinned. 'Since we have that sorted, I'll remind you that I consider getting you back home safe and sound is my responsibility, irrespective of what number date this is.'

Allie managed a smile. 'Okay. As long as

you'll agree that it's also my responsibility to get *you* back home safe and sound. Which in this instance probably involves handing over the car keys.'

'Agreed. Mutual accountability.' He let go of her hand and the car rocked slightly as he squeezed through into the back seat. 'Shift over.'

Allie undid her seat belt, sliding over into the passenger seat. Zac moved forward again, settling himself behind the wheel. 'Ready to go?'

He drove slowly towards the highway, coming to a stop when a couple of kangaroos decided that it would be a good idea to race them, and then gave up when Zac refused to take up the challenge.

'You can't outdrive a kangaroo.' He flashed her a smile. 'Just give them the road and let them get out of the way…'

'Maybe I shouldn't have been quite so ambitious. No streetlights makes the headlights on their own really spooky.'

'Yeah, I don't know anywhere in London that gets completely dark at night, there's always a bit of light coming from somewhere. But you chose a great place for a date and we'll be back on the highway in a minute.' He was relaxed and easygoing, and seemed to have forgotten all about Allie's sudden panic. When they arrived back at the apartment he didn't delay on

the doorstep though and had his keys out ready
to let them inside. Allie supposed that since this
was the second date…

He closed the door behind them and she
caught his hand. This time she felt a lot more
confident about what should happen next.

'Thank you. I had a wonderful evening.' She
reached up, clasping her hands behind his neck,
wondering if Zac would take the initiative this
time and kiss her.

'So did I.' She felt his hands, gentle on the
back of her waist. Not moving, not pulling her
close. That was what she liked about Zac. He
generally gave her plenty of space but when he
did touch her he owned the gesture. Ready to
change it if it wasn't what Allie wanted, and
never pretending that it was anything other than
what it was.

She stared up into his eyes, and he returned
her smile. Then he gently brushed his lips
against her cheek, murmuring quiet words
against her skin. 'I'd really like to kiss you.'

'I'd like that too.'

This time he was more confident. His kiss
was right on the edge of searching and domi-
nant, turning her knees to jelly. But Zac's gentle responsiveness still allowed Allie to feel that
everything which happened between them was

her choice. She moved closer, holding him tight, feeling his strong body taut against hers.

He drew back, his gaze telling her everything that she didn't dare say. Then he kissed her again, this time a light rhapsody of pleasure on her lips. His gentle goodnight sent her upstairs to her room still buzzing with feelings that only a wide sky and the universe could contain.

CHAPTER TEN

AFTER A LATE NIGHT Zac woke late. He'd needed the sleep, but he also needed exercise, balance and the cooling rush of water against his skin, to rid him of the sensual drowsiness that owed more to last night than it did this morning. Mark had already gone inside to open up the shop, and Zac decided to take a swim.

He arrived back in the apartment an hour later, the muscles in his shoulders now looser and aching a little from the amount of exercise he'd put them through. Allie was sitting at the breakfast bar with her laptop open in front of her and a cup of coffee to keep her company.

'Hey there. What are you up to?' He went to the fridge, taking out some fruit to chop and mix with a bowl of granola.

'I'm just looking for some websites to recommend to Carly. I mentioned that there were a few that had helped me, but she won't go onto the web and find them herself.'

'I can see her point. How have things been going with her?' Zac flipped on the coffee machine.

'Good. Now that she's ready physically to be discharged, Philippa and I are working on some of the things she'll be facing when she goes home. It's been really helpful for the three of us to discuss that. I think we've all learned something.'

'And you think she's ready to start going back on the internet now?'

Allie turned the corners of her mouth down. 'I'm not sure that *ready* is quite the word. But it's a fact of life, the same as going back to college when Carly knows that everyone will have seen those pictures. If we can help her feel safe and protected while she reclaims her space, that's really the best we can hope for at the moment.'

Maybe now was the time for Zac to say something. Maybe not…

'So… Tell me more.' He sat down opposite her at the breakfast bar and took a sip of his coffee. 'I'm interested.'

Allie shrugged. 'There's not much more to tell, really. The one thing that the internet's really good at is sharing—information, images and so on. I learned that to my cost, and I've always felt that I wanted to take a part of it back.'

'That's a tall order.'

'Yes, but knowing that there may be images out there which I never wanted to share is a pretty tall order as well. I can try to get things taken down, but it doesn't always work. I reckon that maybe the thing that does work would be to make my own voice heard, but I'm not sure how to do that.'

Zac stirred his granola thoughtfully. She'd said something of the sort before. And if he didn't say what was on his mind now then he was going to have to forget all about the idea.

'You mean your own website?'

Allie puffed out a breath. 'That seems a bit grand. It's well beyond my technical capabilities as well.'

'I know how to make a website. It's actually really easy.'

She stared at him, shaking her head. Then she frowned. This was a *no*, then.

'When you say easy…?'

'How many times have you seen me messing about with computers?'

Allie shrugged. 'Never. But I've only been here for three weeks.'

Three weeks that felt like a lifetime.

'That's pretty representative. When I was a teenager I didn't do social media because I didn't have anyone to socialise with. I used the internet for my studies a lot but that was it. The same when I went to medical school. And when I came here… I just wanted to experience life—the kind you can reach out and touch. I've got my own website, though.' Zac couldn't help feeling a touch of pride at the achievement.

'You have? How come…?' Understanding dawned on Allie's face. 'Does this have anything to do with those mysterious lunchtime and after-work meetings with Jack in the rec room. That I never get invited to?'

Zac nodded. 'I had to get him out of his room and communicating with the real world. So we did a deal. I've been telling him how rehab works and giving him some things to read, and he's taught me how to make my own website. Doing it in the rec room has been really good for him, people get interested and he's started to make friends. He's been exercising a lot more as well.'

'Yes, I noticed that. The muscles in his leg are starting to get stronger…' Allie fixed him with a questioning look. 'Did you do this so that you'd know how to make me a website?'

He hadn't really expected her not to ask. Allie was perceptive enough to understand most things about any given situation and Zac had only justified not telling her about this by promising himself that he'd be honest if it ever came to the crunch.

'It was a good way to get Jack moving around again. And since you'd been talking about taking the things that had been stolen from you back again, it seemed to me to be a good skill to have. If you ever needed it.'

'Two birds with one stone, then.'

Zac shrugged. 'I wouldn't quite put it like that. But yes, I suppose so.'

'And if I'd never mentioned it?' Allie clearly wasn't about to let him off the hook as easily as she might have done.

'Then I wouldn't have said anything about it. I'd have reckoned I'd learned something, and that it had done Jack good as well.'

She stared at him. And then she started to laugh. Zac didn't quite know how to respond to that.

'Zac…!' Her shoulders were shaking, and she clapped her hand over her mouth.

Okay. He hadn't thought that this was particularly funny. Zac picked up his empty cup, emptying the dregs of coffee into the sink and switching the machine back on. Maybe they both needed a few moments.

'Zac… Come here.'

He turned and walked back over to the breakfast bar.

Allie stretched out her hands, taking his. 'Zac, that's the nicest, sweetest thing anyone's ever done for me.'

'And the funniest?' That hurt a little, and Zac wasn't sure why.

Allie must have seen his discomfiture, and her face straightened suddenly. 'I wasn't laughing at you, Zac, I was laughing at me. I came all this way, thinking that Australia had to be far enough to go to get away from everything that had happened, because I couldn't run any further. And then I met you and I'm beginning to feel that I can do what I wanted to all along, stop running and fight back.'

From somewhere, deep in his past, his mother's laughter echoed in his head. The way he'd tried so hard to please her, and been met with nothing but derision. So different from Allie, who had every reason to be bitter, but had somehow retained the ability to love.

'I misjudged you.' Zac turned the corners of his mouth down, wondering how he was going to make this up to Allie.

'If you mean that you judged me by the way you've been treated in the past, then that's not your fault. I'd should have been more thoughtful. I will be in future, because I want to earn your trust.' Her gaze searched his face.

He let go of her hands, leaning over the breakfast bar to kiss her cheek. It felt so soft against his, so warm, that he couldn't draw back. 'You have that already.'

She turned her head slightly, whispering in his ear, 'So what were you saying about a website?'

In other words, Allie trusted him too. Zac smiled, whispering back, 'Think about it. Let me know what you decide.'

They spent more than twice the amount of time in the supermarket than Zac usually allocated for his weekly shop, because Allie was still intent on examining everything that was new and different. It was twice as much fun too, as was dropping into the shop to drink tea with Mark and Naomi afterwards.

'A paddleboard's an investment,' Mark told her sternly as she examined the display. Zac would have characterised it more as something to have fun with, and Naomi's elbow in his ribs indicated her agreement.

'That's the best one!' Izzy piped up, and Allie looked down at her.

'Why's that, Izzy?'

'Because it's yellow.'

Allie squatted down on her heels next to the little girl. 'Do I have to wear yellow as well?'

Izzy thought for a moment. 'You can wear a

yellow T-shirt with a wiggly blue stripe on it.' She described her current favourite from her own collection of T-shirts.

'Sounds good. It's nice to have something that matches.' Allie looked up at the paddleboard.

'The valve on this one is rather more robust. Saves time when you're inflating it…' Mark tried to restore a more serious tone to the process. 'And it's well priced.'

'Dad!' Izzy pushed at her father's leg, trying to move him out of the way. 'It's not yellow!'

Mark scratched his head thoughtfully. 'Yeah. There is that to it.'

'You don't have to buy one now,' Naomi called over to Allie. 'Borrow mine, I'm not using it. Too busy with the next generation of surfers.' She grinned at the baby bouncer, where Finn was waving his arms ferociously.

Mark nodded. 'That's the thing to do. Then you'll know if you want to keep going with it.'

Zac kept his own disagreement with the idea to himself. If Allie had a board of her own she'd use it and going out onto the water seemed to him to be one more step towards a place where she could feel and appreciate the world around her. But he'd be gone soon, and she had to find her own way.

Not everything was about healing, though. Some things you just had to do because you wanted to do them, which in Zac's experience was part of the healing process too. A couple of other customers, clearly serious surfers, had caught Mark's attention and Izzy followed him over to give her own opinion of their choice.

'She's getting to be a handful, isn't she?' Zac grinned at Naomi.

'You don't know the half of it.' Naomi smiled back. 'They talk about the *terrible twos* but just wait until you have a four-year-old.'

Zac had never envisaged that. He loved Izzy, but had never really imagined he'd want to be part of a family again. But somehow, that solid determination that had grown in his heart, the feeling that he'd do anything to make Allie happy even if it meant walking away and leaving her here… That was family, wasn't it? Wanting the best for someone, however much it cost?

Izzy ran over to him, looking up expectantly. Now that Mark was involved in a conversation about the wicking properties of various materials, which didn't appear to take account of their colour, she was getting bored.

'Want to go down onto the beach, Izzy?'

The little girl started in an expression of delight, looking pleadingly up at her mother, and Naomi grinned.

'Haven't you got something to do, Zac?'

'Yeah.' He lifted Izzy up in his arms and she

hung on tight to his T-shirt in an indication that whatever it was he had to do, she'd be coming along to help. 'I'm thinking of going down onto the beach…'

'Sandcastles?' Allie had been lingering by the paddleboards, still sorting through them, but she looked round suddenly.

'*Plee-ee-ase*, Mum.'

'Okay, Izzy.' Naomi shot him a grateful smile. 'Drop in for lunch on the way back, eh?'

Allie and Izzy had embarked on an ambitious sandcastle project, which had temporarily sapped Izzy's excess of energy. Zac carried the little girl up the hill to Mark and Naomi's house, Allie stopping to admire the carefully tended waratah bushes.

'Are we staying for lunch?' Seeing himself and Allie as a unit which made its decisions together was becoming more and more natural.

'If you want. I'd like to see your website, though…' Allie looked up at him questioningly.

Somewhere between paddleboards and sandcastles, she'd made her decision. Zac grinned down at her.

'Right then. Prepare yourself to be impressed. Jack's done a really good job with it.'

He gave their apologies to Naomi, promising to drop in again soon, and tried not to rush

Allie back to the apartment before she changed her mind. But she seemed enthusiastic enough for the both of them, waving away his offer of something to eat first as she sat down at the breakfast bar and opened her laptop. Zac typed the address into her browser, hitting the enter key.

'Zac! That's amazing!' The entry page consisted of a picture that Zac particularly liked. Mark had caught him right at the head of a large wave, a plume of spray following his trajectory.

'Only time I ever managed to do that without falling off. You have to scroll down.'

Allie nodded, clearly having already seen the down arrow at the bottom of the picture. Jack had told him that people would expect that and know how to navigate without being told. Allie studied the picture a little more closely and then started to scroll.

She didn't take her eyes from the screen, finding the menu without any trouble at all and tapping first on the *About Me* icon and reading through the text that Jack had made him write. Then she moved onto the surfing section, which largely consisted of images from his phone. Zac decided to leave her to it and that sandwiches were a good idea, since Allie was clearly reckoning on taking her time with this.

'Who's *InternetWarrior2*?' She'd clearly

worked her way down to the comments section of the page.

'That's Jack. See, *InternetWarrior1* has liked the comment. That's his girlfriend.'

'That's sweet. And I suppose *SurfinDoc* is you, is it?'

'How did you guess?'

Allie grinned. 'The heavy-handed hint that he needs to do his exercises before he'll be ready to surf gives you away. You could be a bit more easy-going, you know.'

Zac shrugged. '*InternetWarrior1* gave me a like. So did *WarriorMum*.'

'I suppose his mother knows best.' Allie made the leap from real life, where Jack's mother was a neat, friendly women who wouldn't say boo to a goose, to her internet persona without any apparent difficulty.

By the time he'd slid the plate of ham and cheese sandwiches and a mug of coffee over the breakfast bar, Allie had been through the page where Zac talked about his work as a doctor, and was clicking on the link which gave hints and tips on water safety.

'There's nothing there!'

'That's the most important part of it, so I'm thinking about what I want to say. What do you reckon?'

Allie reached for a sandwich. 'I think it's

great. It looks really professional and I certainly wanted to keep reading. But be honest, Zac. How much of this is your work and how much did Jack do?'

'Jack showed me how to do it, but all the words and pictures are mine, and I chose the template and set up the pages. I had to go back with some questions, of course, but I know the answers to them now.'

'And the comments section?' Allie had seemed particularly interested in that.

'That comes with the template. You just have to select what elements you want on the page.'

'And how long did this all take you?'

'Jack and I got the general shape of it really quickly, in our first session in the rec room. I spent a bit more time getting everything right in the evenings, after you went to bed.'

'Well, I'm impressed. I know lots of people have websites, but I'd never thought much about how they did it…' Allie turned the corners of her mouth down.

'Too busy in the real world.' An image of the Allie who worked hard and played hard, seemingly without a care in the world, hit him. Two years ago, Zac had felt an obscure longing to be a little more like her, not so much because he wanted to change, but for the opportunity it might give to enter the circle of light that always seemed to surround her.

They'd both changed. His own life had moved on when he'd realised that he needed to change for himself and not anyone else. Allie's… He wouldn't wish that change on anyone, even if it had started her on the long road that led here.

'I didn't need a website then. I need one now.'

Zac thought about the proposition. 'But do you *want* one? It's a big commitment.'

She shrugged. 'I don't know if anyone's even going to read it. I'm not sure if that even matters.'

'You just want to say it?' Allie gave him a silent nod. 'That's okay, but what if people *do* read it? Can you be there for someone like Carly, who might find the site and need help? And what if someone comes on your site and doesn't agree with you?' Jack had told him all about trolling and Zac didn't want to think about that right now. That would add an even greater dimension to Allie's pain.

'It'll be my site. Presumably I can delete comments?'

'Yes, but you've got to look at them first. Don't get me wrong, Allie, I'll help the best I can with whatever you want to do. That's why I did this in the first place. But I'm not going to pretend that it'll be easy. Getting up the courage to say what you want to say is just the beginning. And you know better than I do that what goes onto the internet is difficult to erase, so once you start it's not necessarily that easy to go back again.'

'Don't make it sound too much like a walk in the park, will you?' Allie's rather feeble joke fell flat and a tear rolled down her cheek. All of her enthusiasm, all of that precious glow, was gone now. He'd burst that bubble as efficiently as his mother had stamped on all of his own enthusiasms.

'Allie, if you really want to do this, then I'm with you all the way.' He reached forward, wiping the tear away. 'I truly believe you can do it, but I won't lie to you and tell you it's going to be easy.'

He saw her hand fist in her lap. Allie was going to fight back. It occurred to Zac that all his parents had ever wanted was to subdue his wants and needs with theirs, and the fierce excitement that he felt at Allie's defiance freed him from the nagging worry that his actions owed anything to theirs.

'Don't run away with the idea that this is all your idea, Zac. I've been thinking about something like this for a long time. Now's the time for me to do it, and if I have you to thank for that then…' she shrugged, throwing up her hands in an expression of frustration '…thank you. And if you don't help me set it up, then you're in *real* trouble.'

Zac couldn't help grinning at the thought that somehow he'd played a part in bringing her to this *right time*. 'What kind of trouble?'

'Trouble you won't like.' Allie smiled suddenly, leaning forward to plant a kiss on his cheek.

'I'll warn you now that I can stand any amount of that kind of trouble…'

Allie knew her power over him, and she no longer seemed afraid of it. Zac wasn't afraid of it either. He knew that she'd tell him what she wanted and that she wouldn't break if he pushed her a little. He kissed her, his lips lingering on hers to explore the exquisite sensuality of her response.

'I could pack my bags and go to live in the hospital accommodation…' Allie's threat was accompanied by the sweetest of smiles imaginable.

'You'd be miserable there.' Zac caressed her cheek with his fingertips.

'Yes, I'm sure I would. But I've made up my mind and I'm going to stop at nothing, Zac…'

If only they had more time. Zac would be here for another two weeks, and then he was off to

Queensland for a week, before flying home to England. But Allie knew that trying to force the pace between them wouldn't work. She'd be fearful and ashamed of her own body, and he was bound to know it, however hard she tried to hide her feelings from him. She'd become practised in smiling and keeping going, even though she was dying inside, but this relationship with Zac didn't allow anything but complete honesty.

But there were plenty of things they *could* share. Things that seemed to demand the same trust and the same kind of caring and sharing as making love. And, strangely, she and Zac were now strengthening their relationship in the one place that Allie had thought she might never be at peace with. The internet.

He'd shown her the site that Jack had used to construct his website, and Allie had liked a lot of the templates, and the idea that she could incorporate a blog onto her site. By the time the sun started to sink in the sky, Allie had a website.

'What do you reckon, so far?' They'd decided to celebrate with cocktails on the balcony, and the ice clinked in her glass as Allie stirred her drink thoughtfully.

'It's good. I like the idea of having one page for who you are, and another for your personal statement about what happened to you. It makes the distinction between the two clear. And using blogs to cover different aspects of image-based abuse, and your own journey, gives you a forum to update it regularly.' He paused, looking at her thoughtfully. 'It could do with a few photos.'

That was confronting. But it was important to her as well. 'I want to present the image of myself that I've chosen.'

Zac nodded. 'But you're understandably not that keen on a camera lens. What about the one we took last night, with the stars?'

'I can use it? You're in it as well…'

He laughed. 'It's nice of you to ask. Yes, of course you can.'

Allie thought the idea through. 'I'd like to do a blog about the stargazing. What it meant to me to be able to go and do something new, just because I wanted to. But if I can't show my face to the people I'm trying to reach, what kind of message does that give?'

'That you're cautious. The people you really want to speak to will understand that, won't they?'

'Yes, but… Why should I, Zac? Why should I feel I have to hide from a camera?'

'Because it was a tool that someone used to abuse you. If someone's been stabbed, then no one questions it if they're a little wary of kitchen knives. You don't have to do any more than you're comfortable with, Allie, that's important.'

He'd been cautious and given her some good advice. But this didn't feel right.

'Can we take some pictures tomorrow, Zac? Just to try things out, and I'll see how I feel about them.'

'Sure. Any time.'

Allie could feel a frown coming on, and looked down at her drink, stirring it disconsolately. The jangle of the ice cubes didn't seem quite so perfect, suddenly.

'We'll have to do it soon. In another two weeks…' He'd be gone. Allie would be alone here, albeit with a good place to live and new friends close by, which was more than she could have ever expected to achieve in the course of three weeks.

'I was going to ask you about that.' Zac's voice interrupted her reverie. 'I was thinking of giving Queensland a miss and staying here for the extra week before I fly back to London. Would that be okay?'

A jangle of competing emotions left her numb. 'It's your apartment, Zac. Of course you should stay, for as long as you want.'

His gaze caught hers. 'That's not what I meant. I was wondering if I could stay here with *you*.'

It was hard not to just say *yes*—forget about why he'd offered, and just take this extra time with him. Maybe it was pride and maybe caution that wouldn't allow her to.

'It's really good of you to offer, Zac. But I'll be okay here on my own.'

'I know you will.' He puffed out a breath. 'I made a complete hash of asking you out the first time and so I'm going to try and do better this time around. I've really enjoyed spending these last three weeks. I have two more weeks at work and then another week before I go back to London, and I'd like to spend all of that time with you. If you'd like to spend it with me, that is.'

He couldn't make it any plainer, and that was absolutely fine with Allie.

'Yes. I'd like that too, very much.'

Zac grinned. 'Then it's settled. What do you say we finish our drinks, go for a stroll on the beach and then get an early night? Scout out some places for photographs in the morning, eh?'

CHAPTER ELEVEN

ZAC HAD BEEN up early, finding his camera and downloading his own photographs onto his laptop. He left it on the breakfast bar, with a note for Allie, saying that the now empty memory card was for her to use and then keep, then went outside to join Mark on the beach. The waves were small and uneven this morning, and they spent quite a bit of time sitting on their boards and exchanging ideas about where the sandbank might move to next.

He saw Allie walking towards them, chatting to Naomi, who was bringing the children down to play while the beach was still empty. As he waved to them, he heard Mark's voice behind him.

'You're not going into work today, are you, mate?'

The question wasn't entirely unwarranted. Allie was wearing a pair of neat trousers and a long-sleeved blouse, with a pair of low-heeled sandals. She looked as if she was about to go to a business meeting.

'No. Not as far as I know, anyway.' He waited for Allie to pick her way down the beach towards them. He'd leave it to her to explain if she wanted to.

'I hear you're taking photographs,' Naomi greeted him. 'For a blog.'

Zac nodded. Allie clearly hadn't gone into details, but it seemed that she'd decided to start as she meant to go on, and not make a secret of it either.

'I thought some pictures on the beach for starters, maybe.' Allie was pushing her curls behind her ears, in an effort to stop the breeze from catching them.

Zac decided to put his reservations aside. This was hard for Allie, and she didn't need his criticism to make it harder. 'Great. Where do you want to stand?'

'Um...maybe a little further up, so we can get some sand and the sea in?' Allie started to make her way back up the beach, looking for a good spot, and Zac decided to let her go.

'Are we sure about this?' Mark murmured in Naomi's direction and Zac shot him a warning glance. 'What? She just looks a bit uncomfortable.'

Uncomfortable wasn't the word for it. Allie

looked as if she expected a giant octopus to rise up out of the sea and grab her at any moment.

Naomi rolled her eyes. 'This isn't as easy as it looks, Mark. I know *you* don't label people, but there are plenty who do.'

'What's that supposed to mean?'

'People see you with a child, and you're a mum. If you're in a bikini on the beach then they reckon you don't have a brain, just a body. Wear something a bit more businesslike and they take you more seriously, but heaven forbid you're able to do all three.'

Naomi had a point. And this was all about not allowing herself to be defined by the camera for Allie.

'You do all three.' Mark glanced over in his direction for some support and Zac decided that he was going to have to fend for himself in this discussion. Naomi had given him a place to start and he needed to talk to Allie.

He walked over to where she was standing. 'More difficult than you thought it would be?'

She turned the corners of her mouth down. 'Yes. I don't know where to stand or... I couldn't decide what to wear either.'

'And you wanted to look like someone that people would take seriously?'

Allie shrugged. 'I just want people to hear what I have to say.'

'Fair enough. I'm wearing shorts and a rash vest so I suppose you can completely discount anything I've got to offer...'

'It's different for you, Zac.'

'Granted. But I thought that the whole point of this was to be unashamed of who you are, and to show others that they should be too. What was it you told me that Carly had said? About someone who has their photograph taken being called a *subject* when really they're the centre of it all and in charge of everything that's happening.'

Allie dumped the camera into his hands suddenly, turning to walk back up the beach. 'I'm going to change.' She flung the words over her shoulder at him and Zac grinned.

When he turned, he saw that Mark had taken charge of the children and was wandering along the beach chatting to Izzy, and Naomi was making a beeline for him.

'Everything okay?'

'Yep. I was listening to what you said, there.'

Naomi shot him a sceptical look. 'You were?'

'Allie's gone to change. Something a bit more formal. We were thinking that a tiara might give her a bit more gravitas.'

'You'd better be joking, Zac...'

Naomi's mood improved markedly when, ten minutes later, Allie appeared. She was wearing the light cargo shorts that she usually wore for the beach, with a cap-sleeved blouse. Allie always looked stunning, but now she also looked ready for a day at the beach.

'What do you think?' She smiled at Naomi.

'Fantastic.' Naomi handed Allie her sunglasses. 'Want to try these?'

Allie took the sunglasses, and Naomi nodded in approval. Zac wished he'd thought to suggest them, because they offered the sensation of privacy and at the same time suggested free time and a sunny day.

She stood a little stiffly at first, but soon enough Allie started to relax. Zac took plenty of pictures, reckoning that Allie *had* to find one that she liked amongst them, and then a few with Allie and Naomi together, their arms around each other.

'You just need one?' Naomi asked as the three of them sat together, watching Mark dangle his son's feet over the waves that broke gently onto the beach, while Izzy did her best to drench her father and brother.

'I think I'll have another one of me at work. Not actually *at* work, because that's private, but looking like a doctor.'

'Hmm. How do you look like a doctor?' Naomi asked.

'Large hypodermic and an evil grin?' Zac

flopped onto his back in the sand, feeling the sun warm him. 'Or a stethoscope?'

Allie chuckled. 'I think I'll go for the stethoscope.'

'You could borrow Finn and pretend to be examining him if you wanted.' Naomi floated the idea and Allie shook her head quickly.

'Thanks, but it's got to be just me. The blog's about some pretty serious issues. I'm writing an opinion piece and I shouldn't implicate your family in that, especially a child.'

Zac saw a flash of curiosity in Naomi's face. She was obviously wondering what this was all about.

'That's thoughtful. I wish you well with it.' Naomi decided not to ask, and Zac felt the tightness at the back of his neck relax a little.

Maybe Allie was thinking the same as he was. He was faced with the reality of it now, a chance conversation on the beach becoming something that was challenging and painful. Allie was putting herself in the position of having nowhere left to hide from what had happened to her, but he supposed that he was just experiencing the smallest taste of what she'd been living with for the last eighteen months.

'It's about…' Allie whispered the words so quietly that Naomi didn't hear them, her attention caught by Izzy, who had fallen flat on her face in the sand. Naomi got to her feet, walking over to pick her up, brush her down and give her a hug and a kiss, and the little girl scampered back to Mark.

'Can I tell her?'

'You don't have to.' Zac pulled himself up, leaning on his elbow. The moment was gone now, and Allie didn't need to explain herself.

Allie's gaze met his. 'I want to.'

'That's okay too. Naomi and Mark are good people.' He'd known them both for a while now, and he trusted them.

'Sorry…' Naomi was back now, and she plumped herself down on the sand. 'What were we saying?'

'About the blog. It's *my* blog. Zac's been helping me with it.'

'Ah. Nice.' Naomi shot him a bright, approving smile. 'Making good use of your time then, Zac.'

'It's about…'

Suddenly, Allie lost her nerve. Zac opened his mouth, about to direct the conversation away to a less difficult subject, and then he caught sight of Allie's pleading look.

'Back in London…' he started slowly, and Allie gave a small sigh of relief, nodding him on. 'In London, Allie was a target of image based sexual abuse. The perpetrator went to prison, and Allie wants to speak out about what happened to her, in the hope of helping others.'

Naomi's eyes widened in horror. 'Allie...?'

'It was eighteen months ago, now. It's okay...'

'No, it is *not* okay.' Naomi reached out, laying her hand on Allie's arm. 'It really isn't. I'm so sorry this happened to you.'

Tears of relief started to spill down Allie's cheeks.

Naomi spread her arms, enveloping her in a hug. 'I can understand that you don't want to talk about this. But I'll read your blog.'

'Thanks. That's what I want people to do.' Allie took the tissue that Naomi had produced from her pocket and wiped her eyes, smiling now.

'I could email my friends. Tell them to pass the word on?'

'Thanks, Naomi. Read the blog first, and if you agree with what I say and feel you can share it with other people, that would be a big help.'

Zac hadn't thought of that. He'd been so concerned about Allie, so determined that she should be able to have her own voice heard if that was what she wanted, that he hadn't considered who was going to hear it.

'That's a really good offer, eh, Allie.'

Naomi shrugged it off. 'It's the least I can do. Lots of people are worried about this. I hear that being pressured to swap photos is becoming increasingly common amongst teenagers these days. It's one of the gazillion things I worry for Izzy about and if there's anything I can do to help then just shout.'

'Allie didn't swap photographs.' It seemed somehow important to Zac that he should make the point, although he wasn't entirely sure why. 'It was a video taken without her knowledge…'

'I know you're saying that it wasn't my fault, Zac, but you don't need to defend me. If I had known about the video and made it in the expectation of it being private, then my ex still wouldn't have had any right to share it, and the consequences of it would have been equally devastating,' Allie corrected him gently.

'Yeah. You're right, I didn't think. Sorry.'

Naomi had blanched at the mention of the word *video*, and it looked as if she was still coming to terms with that piece of information. But she shot Zac a sudden smile.

'I always thought you had hidden depths, Zac. Good on you.' Naomi gave him an approving nod. 'Mark'll be opening up the shop in a minute and he can manage on his own for a bit. Why don't you both come back to mine, and we can find a blank piece of wall for that doctor photograph. I have chocolate fudge brownies.'

The chocolate fudge brownies seemed to seal

the deal, and if he was honest Zac needed a few calories. Naomi went to fetch Finn and Izzy, while Zac tucked his surfboard under his arm and started to stroll back up to the apartment with Allie.

'You okay with all of this?'

Allie puffed out a breath. 'I feel as if I've just run a marathon, and my knees are still shaking. But yes, I'm better than okay.'

'And you're ready for the doctor photos?'

'Yes. What shall I wear, do you think?'

It was the first time that Allie had asked him that, and it felt like another small step for man and an enormous leap for womankind.

'What you had on earlier is great. Pin your hair back and hang a stethoscope around your neck and you'll look just as you do at work.'

She nodded, laying her hand on his back, even though Naomi and Mark were probably watching. When Zac put his arm around her shoulders she walked a little closer, falling into step with him.

'You smell nice. Like the sea.'

Despite everything, Zac felt suddenly happy. In moments like these if felt as if they could do anything together and Zac's urgent wish to protect Allie gave way to a more potent ambition. He wanted to fight next to her, in the knowledge that they would protect each other.

* * *

It was the closest to someone staging an intervention that Allie had ever experienced. Zac had mentioned that Mark had asked them to pop in on Monday evening, after work. Naomi made tea and the two men sat silently, nodding their agreement while Naomi spoke for all three of them.

They all admired her for standing up for what she believed in and wanting to help others. Both Mark and Naomi had read every word of what she'd written on the site, after she'd given Naomi the address and the password to view it, and they both believed in what she was doing. But she didn't need to stand alone. They were her friends, and if Allie would agree to add a picture of all four of them on the beach together they'd be honoured.

Allie cried, and Naomi produced a box of tissues out of nowhere, pushing it towards her. 'Think of it like this. You're showing that you have friends who support you. People need to know that too.'

'You're sure?' Allie looked around the group for reassurance and Zac rolled his eyes.

'We're sure. If you need written confirmation, we're happy to provide it. In large letters in the sand.' He gave her that irresistible grin of his, and Allie laughed through her tears.

By Wednesday the site was finished. Allie had asked Naomi for honest comments, and she'd made a couple of suggestions that Allie really liked. All four of them had drawn up a list of friends that they could email, to try and spread the word about the site. But the most touching thing, the thing that always made her smile, was the photograph at the bottom of the *About Me* page. Allie and Naomi, standing on the beach together, with Zac and Mark on either side of them, Zac's arm around her shoulders and Naomi's around her waist.

Allie and Zac walked up to the house at the top of the hill, Zac carrying his laptop and Allie a bottle of iced champagne. Zac ceremoniously removed the password from the site, making it officially live, and they all sent their emails. Then Zac popped the champagne cork while Mark fetched some glasses, so they could drink a toast together to the success of Allie's new venture.

'Now we wait.' Zac put his arm around her shoulders as they walked back down to the apartment.

'I'm not expecting miracles. Maybe a few people will see it as a result of our emails, but I don't mind if I'm talking to an empty room. I've done it, and that's the main thing.'

Zac nodded. 'We'll see. We've worked pretty

hard over the last few days—you fancy catching a movie tomorrow evening?'

'Yes, that would be great. Something to look forward to.'

If one man's hope could do anything to drive a website's stats up, then Zac reckoned that Allie's site would have garnered about a thousand hits by now. They hadn't had time to look at the site on Thursday morning before work, but Allie had switched her phone on during their coffee break and it had started to chime furiously.

'What's that?'

'I set the first blog post up so that I'd get an email when someone commented.' Allie was scrolling furiously. 'I've got over fifty unread emails here, look.'

Zac leaned over to see her phone, his heart suddenly thumping in his chest. He knew he'd wanted this for Allie, but he didn't realise how much. She'd got to the bottom of the list and was smiling.

'Ah! My first comment is from *Surfin-Doc*. He's a pretty nice guy. And then there's *Naomi1357* and *Mark2468*.'

'Hardly imaginative.' Zac tried to curb his glee. They had to go back to work in a minute.

'Oh, shush, Zac. It's really sweet of them.'

Allie started to scroll back up again. 'I don't recognise any of these names—who *are* they all?'

'Um—stop, that's a guy I know who used to work here and moved to Melbourne—Geoff Andrews.'

She opened up the email, scanning the text quickly. 'That's a really good comment. He makes some great points about how health professionals can support people who've been abused.'

'Yeah, Geoff's a nice guy. His wife teaches at a high school, so I wouldn't be surprised if she's commented as well... Allie, I'm sorry, but we've got to get back to work. We can read them all at lunchtime...'

By the time they managed to get away for a late lunch, there were more comments. Allie worked her way down all of them, liking each one, and added her own comment thanking everyone for their interest, and saying she was overwhelmed by the response.

'That'll do it. People like an acknowledgement.' She took a bite from her sandwich, jumping as yet another email pinged into her inbox. 'This is getting crazy.'

Zac nodded, smiling at her. He'd wanted this so much, but now that there were more comments than he'd ever dared hope for, he was afraid that they would overwhelm Allie.

Careful what you wish for...

Zac had been wishing for a great deal lately. He knew that his relationship with Allie had to end, but he was recklessly moving ahead, as if he'd never heard the word *loss* before. And now the website was threatening to overwhelm Allie. But he couldn't bring himself to regret any of it, because he'd never felt quite so alive. He was on a rollercoaster and the only choice available to him now was to hang on.

'What do you say we give the pictures a miss tonight, to give you a bit of time to respond to this?'

She thought for a moment. 'I have to keep this sustainable. I've got to work as well and I could spend for ever getting into discussions with everyone. I'll like things and drop in with a few general comments, but I can't reply to everyone individually, there are only so many ways of saying thank you. I'll post again at the weekend as I'd intended, and if you still want to go to the pictures tonight…?'

'That's a great plan, Allie. You need to keep some time for yourself. And I'd love it if you'd come to the pictures with me tonight.'

CHAPTER TWELVE

WHAT WAS IT they said? Careful what you wish for? The number of comments coming in had subsided after the first day, and Allie spent the day on Saturday taking a tour of central Sydney to see some of the sights with Zac. They had a great time, and when they got back home their kisses were sweeter than ever. Everything was going well and the only cloud on the horizon was that Zac would be going back to London soon.

The second post on her blog had already been prepared and scheduled to post on Saturday evening. Allie had switched off the email alerts that flooded her inbox, in favour of carving out an hour every day to go through them all and write a comment at the bottom thanking everyone for their thoughts.

Then, on Sunday morning, the first challenge came. Luckily, Allie spotted it while Zac was out surfing, and he never saw her reaction. It was just one line, but a cold hand seemed to close around her heart, squeezing hard.

Letting someone take videos of you is just asking for trouble.

For a moment, she was right back where she'd started. Humiliated and afraid, wanting to run to her room, lock the door and cower there. Allie slammed the lid of her laptop closed, shaking.

She could delete that comment. Make it go away. She opened her laptop again, scrolling down a little further, and began to realise that she didn't need to do anything. Five replies did it all for her, explaining why the comment was so hurtful and wrong, and defending her.

'Thank you. *Thank you!*' She sent the thought out into the ether, and then typed her own comment, thanking those who had spoken up for her and closing down that thread. All the same, she still felt sick to her stomach. She decided she'd done enough for today, and opened her email to see if there was anything there for her.

Then she saw the email, and Allie's blood ran cold. It was from one of the nurses at the hospital in London, who started off by saying she'd got Allie's email address from an old round robin invitation for birthday drinks. Anya Patel congratulated her on her new website, and thanked her for standing up to be counted. On behalf of herself and three friends, who had never had the courage to come forward and say that they too had been victims of the group who'd shared Allie's video…

'Hey there.' Allie jumped, slamming her laptop closed, as she heard Zac's voice. 'We caught a few good ones this morning…'

'You did?' Allie forced a smile.

'Are you okay?'

He looked so carefree, tanned and handsome, his clothes dried by the sun. Zac was golden at any time but right now he seemed almost gleaming. She couldn't spoil that.

'Yes, fine. I'm just a bit tired, we walked an awfully long way yesterday.'

Zac grinned at the memory of it. Allie had carefully stowed the day away in her cache of treasured memories, but it felt as if this morning had warped even that.

'You looked as if you'd just seen a ghost when I walked in.' She couldn't escape his gaze now. Perceptive and yet forgiving. As blue as the sea, and about a hundred times more inviting. And she didn't have an answer for him.

'Okay. I could go upstairs and grab a shower. Make some breakfast and maybe go down and get a paper and read it. Any time you'd like to share I'll stop what I'm doing…'

'It's really nothing, Zac.' And it wasn't fair to share this with him. Zac deserved only sunny days, blue skies with no hint of cloud.

'Now I *know* it's something.' He frowned. Try as she might, it seemed that Zac wasn't going to allow her to save him from this.

'Could I have a hug?'

He nodded, walking over to where Allie was sitting at the breakfast bar. Surrounded by the intoxicating mix of his own scent and that of the sea and feeling his arms around her strengthened Allie's resolve. Zac didn't deserve the fall-out from this when he'd done so much to give her back her voice. More than that—she loved him and couldn't bear to hurt him.

'I never really said this. But I have a lot to thank you for, Allie.'

'Me?' Allie didn't know how to reply to that. 'Why would you want to thank me?'

He looked down at her, holding her tight in his gaze. 'You really don't know, do you? For your kindness and your respect. Your bravery. I used to think that functioning well in the world was as much as I could expect, but you've taught me to want more. I won't forget that.'

'I don't think I taught you anything that you didn't already know, Zac.'

'That's where you're wrong. I care about you

and that makes me bold. And it's why it hurts when you shut me out.'

Allie shook her head. 'You don't need to keep supporting and protecting me.'

'No, I don't. I want to, though. I want to share whatever's bothering you as well.'

He'd turned the tables on her, in the most loving way possible, and now Allie had no choice.

'There was quite a negative comment on the blog this morning. I felt really bad about it and then I saw that people had defended me, telling the person who posted it exactly why they were wrong in saying what they did.'

'That's…really upsetting. And really nice, all at the same time.'

'Yeah. I'm going to concentrate on the really nice part of it.'

'And…?' Zac knew this wasn't all of it.

Allie heaved a sigh. 'I got an email, from someone I used to know at work. I can't tell you who, because it must have been really hard for her to write to me, and I have to respect the confidence.'

'Understood. Can you tell me what it said? I'd keep that to myself, of course.'

'I think you must, Zac. However angry it makes you.'

He nodded. 'Fair enough. We can be angry together, eh?'

Allie took a moment to gather her thoughts. 'The person who wrote to me said that she'd been a victim of the group that shared my video. There are three others as well, who didn't come forward.'

She felt Zac catch his breath. 'There are more?'

'At least four. And they've been bearing this weight all of this time, without any support from the hospital. I had that, at least.'

'And you've replied to the email?'

'Not yet. I want to get back to her as soon as possible because I know it must have taken a lot to write to me, but I'm not sure what to say.'

Suddenly it was Zac who was clinging to her, needing her support. Allie hung onto him tightly, and he let out a sigh.

'How about asking if she'd like to talk about things? It seems she does or she wouldn't have written to you, and perhaps you could video-conference. You know this person already.'

'Yes, and I think she might be comfortable with a conversation. It's a good idea. I could tell her that if she or her friends do want to talk a little more then I'd like to be there for them, whenever they're ready.'

'Just as long as you're ready.' The balance tipped again and now Zac was supporting her.

'I can do this. I've learned a lot from working

with Philippa and sharing my own story with Carly and listening to hers. A lot of the things that Carly says strike a chord with me, and I think we've both realised that we're not alone.'

'Why don't you write back now then and I'll make some breakfast?'

'Sounds good. Then we'll spend a lazy day on the beach, being good to ourselves. And each other, of course.'

Zac smiled that warm golden smile of his. 'That sounds really good to me.'

One of the nice things about working with young adults was that they were challenging and demanding, a whole complex bag of medical and emotional issues to solve. Another nice thing about them was that some days they did your job for you.

Jack had made a lot of progress and had been discharged to a rehab facility, but he still messaged the friends he'd made here at the hospital, and Zac had made time to pop in and see how he was doing. Corinne was recovering well, but still found any exertion difficult and was being kept in the hospital because there were concerns that her heart might have been affected by the massive trauma that her body had been through. But she'd struck up a friendship with Carly, who came back to visit her regularly. The two young women were spending time together, providing much-needed companionship for each other.

Zac seemed to navigate the complex web of new friendships and new challenges, ever-changing personalities and needs with ease. That was deceptive, and Allie knew that giving each of his patients the impression that he had all of the time in the world for them was the result of a great deal of hard work, and sometimes a juggling act. But this afternoon everything seemed to have fallen into place. The ward was quiet and running like clockwork, which was just as well because Allie was exhausted from four late nights in a row.

Carly was in Corinne's room, the two of them watching afternoon soap operas on TV. Allie had sat down for just one minute to go through Corinne's notes…

Then she felt Zac shaking her. She opened her eyes with a start, suddenly fully awake. Zac was only moments ahead of the head of the unit, Dr Jamieson, who'd stopped outside Corinne's room to talk with the ward manager.

'Ah, I've been wondering where you were, Dr Maitland-Hill.' Dr Jamieson ran the unit like a precision machine, which made everyone's lives easier, but sleeping on the job wasn't included in his policy that his staff should have time to spend with their patients.

'We've been going through our ongoing recovery plans.' Corinne had hastily switched off the TV and answered for Allie. 'Carly and I are keeping in touch after I leave here, so that we can give each other a bit of encouragement.'

Quick thinking. Allie shot Corinne a grateful look, hoping that her hair wasn't as wild as it usually was when she woke up in the morning, and wondering whether she might become invisible in the now slightly crowded room.

'Excellent.' Dr Jamieson seemed pleased. 'It's nice to see you again, Carly. Do either of you have any concerns that you'd like to raise with me?'

That was Dr Jamieson's purpose in being here. He was an advocate of the principle of management by walking around, and made sure that staff and patients all saw his face at least once a day, and knew that they could speak directly to him if they wanted to.

'No. Everything's fine.' Carly was beginning to speak up for herself a bit more now, and Dr Jamieson's nod of approval showed that he was aware of the work that had gone into that.

'Right then. Nothing for me to do here.' Dr Jamieson beamed at them both. 'I'll be seeing you tomorrow, Corinne.'

No doubt he would. Allie made a pledge to herself that she'd contrive to be awake. Dr Jamieson swept out of the room, and Carly and Corinne exchanged amused looks.

'What? We *are* keeping in contact, aren't we?' Corinne grinned up at Zac, who didn't seem to share her amusement. A quick motion of his hand indicated that he wanted to speak to Allie alone.

'I'd better go. I really appreciate the…um… chat.' Allie grinned at Corinne and Carly.

'No trouble.'

Carly reached for the TV remote, and Allie caught Zac rolling his eyes as he left the room. She shot a grimace in Corinne's direction and picked up the tablet that contained her patient notes, tucking it under her arm.

As she followed Zac, she heard Corinne murmur to Carly, 'I'd be aiming for some late nights if I were working with Dr Gorgeous all day…'

'Hmph…' Carly rejected the idea, turning the sound on the television up.

They didn't know the half of it. That was probably just as well, and Allie followed Zac, who was heading along the corridor as if he were on an urgent mission of some kind. He opened the door to the main stockroom, looking around and then motioning her inside. Overreacting much?

'What's going on, Allie?' He folded his arms, his face grim.

'I'm sorry. And thanks for covering for me. It won't happen again.' Allie decided that attack might be the best form of defence. 'But can you honestly say that you've never had an opportunity to sit down for a moment and then fallen asleep at work?'

'When I first qualified and was on call, yes. I can't say I've done it recently. That's not my point, Allie.'

'What *is* your point, then?' Guilt, knowing she'd done the wrong thing, lent a note of irritation to her voice.

'How late were you up last night?'

'Not that late.' Allie had gone to her bedroom to video-conference with Anya, and then written a follow-up email that had taken a while. But she'd been in bed at a reasonable time. 'I just didn't sleep all that well.'

'Yeah, I got that. I heard you getting up at three in the morning and going downstairs, and was awake for half an hour wondering if you'd come back up again…'

She hadn't. Allie's head had been spinning and she'd been pacing around downstairs, trying to work off her agitation.

'What, I'm under surveillance now, am I?'

The look on his face made her regret the words as soon as they left her mouth. 'I'm sorry,

Zac. I didn't mean that. It was a horrible thing to suggest, to you of all people.'

'But that's the kind of thing that happens when you're bone-weary?' His expression had softened a little in the face of her apology.

'I suppose so. But… I can't just leave them on their own with this, Zac. I don't have it in me.'

'I know. But you've been video-conferencing and emailing every evening for the last three days now. You have a demanding job here, and you're burning the candle at both ends. It's not going to work, Allie. You're going to have to find a way to make your website a sustainable effort. And find it quickly.'

She knew that. Zac would be leaving in another ten days' time, and he wouldn't be here to cook dinners and support her in all the other little ways he'd been contriving to help.

'Please don't be so angry with me, Zac…' She couldn't take it right now.

'I'm not angry, I'm worried. We need to talk about this, and find some way through it.'

Actually, Zac didn't need to do anything at all. He could turn his back and walk away, leaving her to try and cope with what seemed to be two jobs in one day. But Zac didn't walk away, not from his patients or from her.

'We'll talk, I promise. I'm really grateful that you're concerned for me, and to tell you the truth I'm concerned for myself. I'll make dinner this evening, and then we'll take a walk on the beach and then get an early night. Tomorrow's Friday and we can talk then.'

'I may confiscate your laptop. And your phone.'

'That's okay. I'd be grateful if you did, actually. There are only so many hours that I can give to the people who've come onto my blog. I almost wish I hadn't done it, or at least left it a while until I was more settled.'

He reached out, his fingers brushing her cheek. All of the warmth, all the feeling that she never wanted to let him go, flooded through her veins.

'No you don't.'

Allie sighed. 'You're right, I don't. It's a lot of work, but I feel that I've finally begun to own myself and what's happened to me. I couldn't have done that without you, Zac. It's your achievement just as much as it is mine.'

He nodded, smiling. 'Heard and appreciated.'

'Are you going to forgive me now?'

Zac chuckled. 'No, I don't think I will until we talk tomorrow and find a way through this.'

A good night's sleep had done wonders. Allie flew through her day's work, and Zac suggested that they catch the food truck on the beach for their evening meal before going back to the apartment for coffee, and to get out of their work clothes. Sitting on the balcony, overlooking the beach, the sound of the sea added a calm to the mood.

'I've got a proposal for you. We'll both have to agree to make it work.' Zac had thought for a while before opening the conversation.

They'd always made their own rules. And maybe Zac was about to come up with another rule that would work better than Allie had ever imagined it might. 'I'm listening.'

He nodded. 'It's clear that you can't go on the way you have been. You could decide to limit the amount of time that you spend on your website, but in practice that's going to be hard because you feel so strongly about the issues it raises and you want to help people. I've assumed that I'll go back to the London hospital when I go home, but I haven't committed myself to that yet.'

Sudden joyous hope made Allie's heart beat faster. Zac was going to tell her he'd stay…

'But…going home's important to you, Zac. You've always said it was the final step in reclaiming your life.' Allie smothered her own selfish wish to say *yes* to the plan before Zac had even had a chance to suggest it. He'd always considered her needs, and she had to consider his.

'Yeah. I could do that now, or I could do it next year. As long as I do it, and I know I will, it's not going to be an issue.'

He was going to ask. They'd live together, here in the sunshine, and in time they'd learn how to make a life together.

'You're sure?' Before she got carried away, Allie had to ask.

'I'm sure.'

A future seemed to be forming, right there in front of her.

Allie swallowed hard. 'Are you saying that you've been considering staying here?' *With me.* Allie didn't dare say the words but it was all she could think about.

'I've been considering a lot of things. What I most want is to be able to stay with you and find out where our relationship might lead but...' He shook his head, as if saying a regretful goodbye to the dream. 'The only thing that I can see working for both of us is that I stay so that you can go home.'

'What? Zac...?' She'd been mistaken, and the world felt suddenly as if it was crashing down, burying her under the rubble of her shattered hopes.

'I've thought about this a lot, and I know two

things for sure. You can't abandon the people back in London who need your help, even if it means you have to tear yourself in half. And this is your chance to make a difference, and to take back everything that's been stolen from you. Your website has shown you can do it. It's just the beginning.'

'But…' Allie brushed a tear away. She couldn't let him see her cry, and Zac mustn't know what had prompted her tears. Hadn't she promised herself that she would never allow a man to humiliate her again?

'I'm moving on here, Zac. There's no way back for me.'

'We can make that way back. I can meet your commitments here, and you'll have the opportunity to go and do something that could put your whole life back in focus. It's a lot to ask of you, but it's not impossible.'

Allie couldn't meet his gaze now, for fear that he'd see what was going on in her head. She was grabbing at straws, trying to find something that would allow them to be together. But, deep down, she knew that Zac was right.

'Can I think about this?'

He smiled suddenly. 'And try to find a way to talk me out of it?'

'Yes, actually. How do you always know what I'm thinking, Zac?'

'Because you know what I'm thinking. Which is why you can't bring yourself to argue with this idea…'

Neither she nor Zac had anything more left to say. They both knew what they had to do, but Allie wasn't ready to agree to it yet. And even though it was Zac's plan, he seemed positively relieved when she brought the conversation to a close by saying she was going out for a walk.

A month ago, she would have gone upstairs and locked herself in her room. But now the need to think brought with it an urge to go outside, and let the open air blow away some of the cobwebs. Maybe some of the bitter disappointment too.

She'd tried to tell herself that she hated Zac, and that he'd turned out to be just the same as James, hurting her and letting her down. But Allie knew that wasn't true. He'd never promised her anything that he couldn't deliver on. And he was right about this. They both needed different things. She needed to go back to London, and he needed to stay here and cover for her at the hospital.

If it meant they had to part, then maybe that was what they both needed to do too. They were both afraid of commitment, and both of them had their reasons to fear promises that couldn't be kept. They didn't have the luxury of time, to allow their relationship to evolve and heal those wounds. They had to act now, before they were ready.

Allie walked for a long time, trying to think of another solution, or at least dispel some of the disappointment that haunted her. When dusk began to fall and she returned to the apartment, she found Zac stretched out on the sofa, fast asleep. He seemed so peaceful, but Allie didn't want him to wake after she'd gone to bed and find she'd left him here.

'Allie…?' He sat up with a start, almost as soon as she touched his shoulder.

'You didn't sleep last night?' Zac had always seemed inexhaustible but tonight he *had* appeared tired. As if his usual spark had gone out.

'No, not much.' He pressed his lips together in a look of regret. 'You're angry with me?'

'Not with you. I'm angry that life doesn't seem to want to give us a break.' And that neither she nor Zac could make the promises that were needed to fight that.

'I've got to believe that it will.' Zac's shrug told Allie that currently he wasn't too sure.

'Me too.' She leaned forward, kissing his cheek. 'I'm going to get an early night, and you should too.'

CHAPTER THIRTEEN

THE WEEKEND HAD been hard. They'd done all of the same things but they'd lost their lustre because there would be no going back on this parting. Zac knew that he'd have to stay in Australia for the next year or put the whole exchange programme into jeopardy. And if Allie went home to London she'd have to stay there to meet the commitments she'd made to the people who she felt she'd left behind by coming here.

But there were no arguments because they both knew this was right. They'd talked again on Sunday afternoon and finally made their decision together. Zac had suggested a clean break, knowing that it would at least spare them the pain of losing a little more each day, and Allie had agreed.

He'd called Dr Jamieson and asked for a meeting with him and the exchange scheme co-ordinator. The four of them sat down together at ten in the morning, Allie looking pale and nervous. Zac explained what he and Allie wanted to do, making it clear that he would stay in his post for the full year, in order to fulfil the contractual commitments that Allie had made. True to form, Dr Jamieson didn't look pleased. He'd never been a man who liked surprises.

'So you've decided this between you.' He frowned. 'Do we have any say in the matter?'

'Of course. Allie needs to go back to London for urgent personal reasons. If you'd like me to stay here to maintain continuity and fulfil the commitments that London's made to the exchange programme, then I'm at your disposal.' The idea that Dr Jamieson might give them both the sack on the spot occurred to Zac and he dismissed it as being far too optimistic.

'Quite honestly, I'm not happy with this, Dr Forbes. We can't have our exchange doctors changing their plans on a mere whim, and since neither of you have given any reasons for Dr Maitland-Hill's return to London then I'm not able to assess them.'

'But in practice it's a good solution, Dr Jamieson.' The exchange scheme co-ordinator was one of the people who knew what had happened to Allie before she'd come here, and had listened with a sympathetic air. 'Zac's record here is exemplary, and we'd be lucky to keep him on here for another year.'

'That's not the point.' Dr Jamieson frowned. 'Reliability is a key requirement and I'm minded to write to London and register my disapproval in the strongest terms—'

'No.' Three heads turned to Allie as she interrupted. 'Dr Jamieson, *I'm* the one who's being unreliable, and Zac's simply offering to regularise the situation.'

'But you've dreamed this plan up together, obviously.' Dr Jamieson seemed only slightly mollified by Allie's defence of him. Zac shook his head in a signal that she didn't need say any more and Allie ignored him.

'I'm sure you're aware of the issue at the London hospital, regarding image-based sexual abuse—about eighteen months ago now.'

'I am.' Dr Jamieson's face softened suddenly.

'I was one of the people who was touched by that…'

Allie told her whole story clearly and concisely, which did nothing to lessen its impact. She'd come so far, and Zac was so proud of her, even if he hadn't wanted her to have to do this.

'This is something I have to do, Dr Jamieson, for my own sake and for the sake of the others who have been involved with this and haven't yet stepped forward. And for the sake of patients like Carly, who've been traumatised by this kind of abuse and who need a practical, joined up response from their healthcare providers. I feel very strongly about this, and I also feel strongly that you're being unfair to Zac. He's done nothing but support me and this hospital.'

Allie stopped, apparently having run out of breath, because she gulped in a lungful of air. Dr Jamieson looked at the exchange scheme coordinator, who gave a slight shrug.

'Go ahead, Dr Jamieson. I'll let you give your views first.'

'Thank you, Sheena.' Dr Jamieson faced Allie. 'Thank you for sharing this with us, and I hope you'll accept my personal apology for putting you into a position where you felt you had to do so.'

Zac wasn't surprised at Dr Jamieson's response. He was outspoken and firm, but he could never be accused of lacking compassion.

Allie smiled suddenly. 'It's all right. I'm learning that this kind of abuse thrives on secrets, and being here has helped me find my own voice. We shouldn't have asked you to accept our proposal without explaining a little more fully.'

Dr Jamieson glanced at Zac and he shrugged. Allie seemed to have this all in hand.

'That's as may be, Allie. Zac, if you're willing to stay on then we'd be delighted to have the opportunity of keeping you for another year. And

Allie, I wish you well. If I can help you in any way, I hope you'll see your way clear to letting me know immediately.'

'You didn't need to do that.' Zac murmured the words to Allie as they left the meeting room together.

'Yes, I really did. I appreciate the gesture, but you were about to take whatever Dr Jamieson said without defending yourself. I want to speak up for people affected by image-based abuse, and I won't have you compromised by its secrets, Zac.'

He nodded. 'Thank you. I had a horrible feeling that he was about to throw the book at me there.'

He felt her fingers brush against his. 'I'm not going to stand aside and let anyone put you down, Zac.'

Warmth penetrated the heavy sadness that Zac had been feeling at this final confirmation of their plan. Allie meant so much to him and what she'd done meant a lot too—she might well have saved him from a serious blot on his copybook, but that didn't matter so much as the fact that she clearly cared enough about him to want to defend him.

'So what would you like to do for the rest of the day? Since we unexpectedly have it to ourselves.' Sheena had suggested that they take the afternoon off, and Dr Jamieson had agreed.

'I suppose that I'd better get my ticket home sorted. That shouldn't take too long though, so perhaps we could take the paddleboards out for a while this afternoon? One more thing I can take back to London with me—a crash course in paddleboarding.'

Zac chuckled. 'I'm glad you have your priorities straight. That definitely sounds like a plan.'

The whole week had been an exercise in priorities and squeezing everything they could from Allie's last few days in Australia. Their last few days together. She'd driven him in to work every morning and met him each evening so that they could spend time together, visiting all of the places that Zac loved and wanted to share with her.

On Thursday evening Allie pulled out her phone as soon as he got into the car. 'I have to ask you this now, because I need to get back to the guy by six-thirty…' She looked at her watch. 'I was thinking of something we might do at the weekend, rather than moping around the apartment and feeling sad.'

Zac had been wondering about that too. 'What have you come up with?'

'There's a log cabin in the Blue Mountains.

We can drive up there on Friday evening and come back on Monday morning, before my flight on Monday afternoon. I managed to find a last-minute cancellation but, as I said, I have to let the guy know soon. And there's a catch.' She squeezed her face into an expression of both apology and…something else. Zac didn't know what.

'What's the catch?'

'It looks beautiful in the pictures, and the area's gorgeous. But there's only one bedroom.'

That didn't sound like much of a problem to Zac, but he had to remember Allie's feelings. And the fact that they'd be on two different continents next week. 'That's not a problem. I'll throw a camp bed into the car and use that.'

Allie pursed her lips. 'Or we could just both use the bedroom.'

Zac shook his head. 'I don't think that's a good idea. A man can only take so much temptation.' He could admit to that now.

'So can a woman. That would be okay.' She was gripping her phone in one hand and the steering wheel in the other, and Zac wondered which of them might shatter under the pressure of her fingers first.

'You're saying…a last weekend? Together?' Against all of his better judgement that sounded wonderful. And perhaps there was a freedom in having no more left to lose.

'I'm saying a last weekend where we can make any memories we want to take with us. Where nothing's planned and we just go with the flow. Talk a bit, and do whatever feels right at the time.'

Zac leaned over, kissing her. 'That sounds perfect, Allie. Make the call.'

Zac had spent one restless night alone, before Allie drove him to work on Friday morning. She'd anticipated his own feeling that memories which centred around the apartment might be too much to bear, and made it clear that the weekend was something separate and very special. Zac had to admit that he was looking forward to the *very special* part.

She picked him up from work, his bag packed and in the back of the car. They headed west out of Sydney and before dark fell they'd found their way to the log cabin, set on top of a ridge, amongst a stunning panorama of wooded peaks.

'We can see for miles!' Allie exclaimed as she got out of the car, stretching her limbs. 'It's so beautiful, Zac.'

He hugged her. 'And we'll have the stars tonight for company.'

'Hmm. They might have to wait their turn. I have *you* for company as well.'

They took their bags inside, finding that the log cabin was small but well equipped and decorated just as beautifully as the pictures on the website that Allie had shown him. She set about making dinner in the tiny kitchen, and they sat down for a leisurely meal outside. Allie was slowing the pace, letting the quiet majesty of their surroundings slowly work its magic, and Zac was on board with that. This weekend wasn't about rushing to do all of the things that they wanted to do before they had to part. It was about getting away from the realities of the world, and taking their time to enjoy whatever the weekend might hold.

They talked for hours, moving inside when the cool of the mountain air started to make them shiver, to sit together by the stove in the cosy wood-panelled living room.

'It's almost nice to be cold, isn't it.' Allie snuggled against him and he laughed.

'Yeah. Particularly when I have you to keep me warm.'

Their talk evolved into a long, slow piece of foreplay, as Allie questioned him about what made him feel good. He told her how the feel of salt water rushing against his body and the roar of the waves had seemed to free him. He described the pleasure he got from feeling her fingertips brush his skin, and when Allie asked he gave her the ultimate power over him and told her what turned him on during lovemaking.

'I never told anyone that before. I'm feeling a little exposed…'

Allie chuckled. 'You're a doctor. You imagine I have no understanding of the physiology of sex?'

Zac resisted the temptation to clamp his hand over his private parts and tell her that they were out of bounds. 'I suppose I'll just have to rely on you to use the information wisely.'

She kissed his cheek, mischief glinting in her eyes. 'Yes, I suppose you will.'

'So I reckon it's your turn now. Since I'm now at your mercy.'

Allie shot him a shy smile, whispering in his ear. Zac chuckled. 'Yeah, I checked too. I think we can both be confident that no one's put cameras anywhere here.'

'That's so sweet of you, Zac.' Allie kissed him. 'It's silly of me…'

'No, it isn't. It makes you feel more comfortable and that's all that matters.'

'Now that we're so close, I'm a little afraid.'

'That's okay too.' Zac knew that Allie was telling him her greatest secrets, and the pleasure that gave him far outweighed anything that she might say. 'Of me?'

'Never of you.'

He smiled. 'That's good to know.'

'I just don't want to spoil things. I've spent eighteen months willing people not to even see me. What happens if you look at me and I panic?'

Zac didn't need to even think about that. 'If it happens, we'll deal with it. All I ask of you is that you tell me if you're feeling uncertain about anything. Otherwise *I* might start to panic.'

'I promise, Zac. You can rely on me to keep that promise.'

Warmth began to spread through his body. Allie knew how much an unbreakable promise meant to him. Maybe this was what they'd really come here for. To give each other these precious gifts.

She slid onto his lap, her legs astride him, her gaze full of tender fire. Like a conquering queen who had cleared every obstacle from their path and who was now claiming what was hers. He *had* been hers, from the first moment he'd seen her.

She kissed him, still holding him tight in her gaze. It was the most intoxicating thing he'd ever experienced, and he slid his hands upwards from her waist, stopping just before his touch met her breasts. Allie shivered, as if she could already feel what he wanted to do now.

'Are we going to do this?' It was okay if her answer was no, but he really hoped it would be yes.

Allie put one hand on his chest, over his heart, and he felt himself give every beat of it to her. Her other hand moved his, and the way she suddenly caught her breath as his fingers closed over the exquisite swell of her breast told Zac that she wanted him as much as he did her.

'Yes, Zac. We're going to do this.'

Every touch. Every move. Zac's gaze never left hers, and she could see her own desire reflected in his. She was already more naked than she'd ever been, and no one could ever take this from her. It was hers and Zac's alone.

When he kissed her, she could feel fire in her veins. And when his hand cupped her breast the delicious ache for him became even more insistent. Then Zac moved, leading her the few short yards to the bedroom.

He switched the lamp on, and the honey shades of the wood turned to gold. Allie sat down on the edge of the bed, but when she reached for him Zac shook his head.

'Don't move.'

He pulled his sweater and shirt off in one

smooth movement, dropping them onto the floor. Then his boots and jeans, and finally his underpants. All of those hours on the beach had left him unashamed of his body, and there were no unnecessary flourishes to hide any embarrassment at being watched. And she *was* watching him.

She nervously tugged at the top button of her cardigan, and he shook his head. 'Don't you want to find out a bit more about me first?'

Allie got to her feet. 'Come here.'

He was within reach now, and she could caress his skin and feel the ripple of muscle as his body reacted to her touch. There was a hungry insistence to his kiss, and when she slid her hands downwards she felt his erection swell at the brush of her fingers.

And he was holding back. Letting her do whatever she wanted with him, and trying to subsume his own desires. That made Allie want him even more.

'Buttons, Zac.' She stood on her toes, whispering in his ear. 'Help me with my buttons.'

His hands were trembling, but he did as he was told. When she stood naked before him, Allie felt no shame, just an overwhelming need to take their lovemaking further. She backed towards the bed, and he bent to pull the covers to one side. She caught his hand.

'I'd like to see you, Zac. Is that okay?'

His grin told her that it was better than okay, and that he didn't want to hide beneath the covers any more than she did. Zac got onto the bed, propping himself up against the pillows, stretching his long legs out in front of him.

'Is that all right?'

'Beautiful. You're beautiful, Zac.' Allie laid her finger across his mouth. She didn't need him to say it back. She knew that he was looking, and the response that he couldn't control told her that he liked what he saw.

She'd left the condoms tucked behind the head of the bed, and when Allie leaned forward to get them she felt his hand slide gently along her thigh.

'We're not quite ready for that yet, are we?'

She was ready. He was definitely ready. Allie clutched at the condoms as he pulled her down onto his lap. He moved her astride him again, and set about redefining the word *ready*.

'Zac! *Please...*'

If she'd known that was the word he'd been waiting for Allie would have said it a little sooner. But then she wouldn't have known exactly what one man could accomplish with just his fingers and his mouth. She felt him prise the packet of condoms from her hand and let go of them gratefully.

Zac kissed her as she carefully guided him inside. His arm coiled around her waist and he began to move, gently at first and then faster and harder, encouraged by her garbled words of encouragement.

Then she felt it. The first tremulous signs of an orgasm. Allie had wondered if she'd ever have the courage to experience this again with any man, and she whimpered with longing, not just for Zac but for what they'd made together. She squeezed her eyes shut, trying to concentrate on the feeling and nurture it, afraid that her body might betray her. And then she felt Zac still suddenly.

'No, Zac. Don't stop. I don't want you to stop…' She felt her hand fist against his shoulder.

Then he moved again, holding her tight in his arms as he flexed his hips. He'd learned her body now and knew just what to do, and the feeling was back again, stronger and more insistent. Allie almost wept with relief, clinging onto him as waves of sensation crashed through her. She collapsed against him, her heart pounding.

'Are you okay?'

No, actually. He'd given her everything and taken so little for himself. But a *no* was likely to give Zac the wrong impression.

'Okay doesn't cover it, Zac. I loved every moment.'

'So did I. Do you want to rest now?'

She lifted her weight from his body, pushing at his shoulder until he slid himself down on the bed. 'You've just given me something that I didn't think I'd ever want from a man again. We're not done yet, Zac.'

That pleased him, and he smiled up at her as she positioned one of the pillows under his head. Then his grin broadened as she reached down, her fingers caressing him.

'I don't need…' His body arched suddenly as she dialled the pressure up a little. 'Yeah. On second thoughts, I do.'

Taking him inside her again was pure pleasure. Moving the way he wanted her to move. Making sure that he felt all of the things that she'd felt so keenly. Zac took it all, pushing hard against her until she came again, just from the pure pleasure of seeing and feeling his arousal.

Then suddenly he flipped her over onto her back. Allie yelped with delight, seeing desire burn bright in his eyes. He tilted her hips, sinking deeper inside, and she felt a deep satisfaction roll over her as he cried out, his limbs shaking.

It was nice that he couldn't speak straight away. She wound her arms around him, feeling the warmth of his skin and the frantic beat of his heart. This was her time to remember him by and it had seared itself into her, becoming a part of her now.

'Allie. This time I'm not asking. I have to rest now.'

CHAPTER FOURTEEN

ZAC HAD WATCHED as Allie took a thin cotton nightshirt from beneath the scattered pillows, pulling it over her head before she lay down with him. In the warmth of the bed, she'd curled her body around his, and he didn't even care that he couldn't feel her skin. Allie had dared so much tonight, and this was nothing.

He had the pleasure of stripping the nightshirt off her again in the morning. They'd found their balance now, trusting each other enough to be able to combine his pleasure with hers. With trust came confidence, and Zac was in no doubt that Allie loved it as much as he did when their lovemaking became bolder and more assertive.

Isolated here, in the spectacular beauty of the mountains, made it easier to feel that time was standing still. There were no more secrets to keep, no promises to break, and that allowed them to take all they could from the forty-eight hours that they did have. But when they loaded their bags into the car, and Allie bade him a tearful farewell from the cabin that had sheltered them from the world, there was no escaping what would come next.

When they arrived home Allie's bags were still waiting for her. There was time enough for lunch, and for Allie to hug Naomi and Mark, and then came the silent journey to the airport. Zac hung onto her hand as they made their way towards the security checkpoint.

'I don't want to go, Zac. I can't…' Now that he could go no further, the realities of their decision seemed to hit home.

'We talked about this, Allie.'

'I know, but can't we talk about it again? Isn't there something we can do?'

'We've made promises. We can't go back on them and…' Zac shrugged '… I don't want you to go back on this, because it's what you need to do.'

She reached up, winding her arms around his neck. 'I really wish that you weren't right.'

'Yeah. Me too.' He kissed her. One last taste of her lips, to hold and to keep with his other memories. 'Allie, it's time now. Let's make a promise to each other, that we'll say goodbye and then walk away. No looking back. We'll just take what we have now.'

Allie heaved a sigh. 'Yes. Yes, that's the best

thing. We'll do that. I'll always love you, Zac. Always…'

He felt his resolve begin to falter. Zac had to do this now, or he'd break every promise he'd made, fall on his knees and beg her to stay. If he did that, he knew that Allie would break her promises, and he would never be able to forgive himself.

'Goodbye, Allie.' Zac turned, forcing himself to walk away. Trying not to think about the look of shock he'd seen in her eyes as she realised that the moment they'd both been dreading had finally come.

Somehow he made it back to his car. The sun seemed harsher now, and the air in the vehicle was stale and uncomfortably hot.

I'll always love you…

Why hadn't he been able to tell Allie that he'd always love her too? Zac pulled out his phone, wondering if his call would get through to her. Just to say those words, as he should have done when he had the chance.

But it was too late. It was the wrong promise to make, one that could only be broken. The road back to Cronulla was the only one left open to him now.

It had been a month, and every single day of it had been hard. Allie had stepped off the plane, fresh tears still in her eyes, and London had seemed very cold and grey. Her flat hadn't been heated for a month, and she'd shivered under her duvet until the central heating finally began to warm the place up. She'd cursed herself for falling in love with the most honourable man she knew, and woken in the night crying.

And then she'd got up and gone to work.

The money she'd saved, by never going out or buying herself anything nice, was standing her in good stead now because Allie had more than six months before she needed to find a job. She'd got in touch with Anya, who had introduced Allie to the three other women from the hospital whose images had been stolen and shared on the internet. She'd knocked on every door, talked to everyone who would talk to her and spent hours on the internet, trying to track down videos and photographs so that they could be reported and taken down. She'd made a nuisance of herself with the HR department of the hospital, who considered that the matter of image-based abuse had been dealt with and was closed, and advised her to let this go and move on.

Then she received a phone call.

'Dr Maitland-Hill.' The woman didn't wait for confirmation. 'I'm Sir Anthony Greve's secretary and he would like to arrange a meeting with you. He is, of course, extremely busy, but I have a free slot in his diary at ten past two this afternoon.'

Sir Anthony Greve, the Chief Executive Officer of the hospital. Allie was either in very deep trouble or this was a breakthrough, and from the tone of his secretary's voice and the specific time slot it sounded like the latter.

'Hold on one moment.' Allie laid her phone down on the kitchen counter, counting silently to ten. That seemed about the right amount of time to consult a diary. 'Yes, I'm free at ten past two.'

'In that case, please come to my office at two…'

There was a pause and Allie raised her eyebrows. Maybe the secretary was consulting her own diary to see if she was free.

'No, I have a note from Sir Anthony saying that he'll meet you for coffee at Sloanes in Mayfair. You know it?'

Yes. Sloanes was a very exclusive restaurant, the booking of which was said to be practically impossible unless you were at least a knight of the realm, or known personally to the management. One of those places that no one ever talked about, and Allie only knew about because several people from the upper echelons of the hospital had been there at Sir Anthony's invitation and the news had filtered down.

'I know it.'

'I'll send you a confirmation and directions, anyway.'

Sir Anthony's secretary rattled off Allie's personal email address for confirmation, and abruptly ended the call.

Was this a joke? Or something more sinister? All the old fears suddenly slapped her in the face. She was being watched. There was a shadowy group of people who wanted to stop her from speaking out, for fear of their own part in the image-based abuse becoming known. If only Zac were here, he'd know what to do.

She finished making coffee and opened her laptop. Several emails pinged into her inbox, one of which was from Sir Anthony's secretary. Clearly what the woman lacked in personal warmth she made up for with efficiency. Allie examined the email carefully, displaying the metadata. The hospital address was genuine, and it all looked legitimate.

This could still be some kind of trap, and it was still impossible to work out where her own paranoia ended and sensible caution began at times. Or she could be in for a polite but firm offer that she couldn't refuse, to shut her website down. That wasn't going to happen. Allie had given up too much for this. An image of Zac, tanned and golden, walking out of the sea, assailed her and she almost wished that Sir Anthony *would* shut her down and pack her off back to Australia in disgrace…

But she had to go. Zac would have grasped the nettle and gone, and the thought gave her courage.

Sloanes was entered via an inconsequential-looking door, in a very select part of Mayfair. It had no need to advertise—anyone who would be allowed to enter would know where it was. Allie was wearing her best suit and coat, which doubtless wouldn't impress anyone, and she arrived early, waiting across the street.

At five past two she saw Sir Anthony walking along the opposite pavement. He stopped at the door, which opened almost immediately, and he gained admittance just as quickly. So at least he was here, which ruled out some of Allie's fears. She shouldn't keep him waiting, and she dodged across the street, thick with taxis and high-end cars.

As soon as she gave her name she was welcomed inside. There was an air of quiet quality about the place, obviously designed to confront anyone who shouldn't be here, and Allie ignored it. One advantage of having been to the most terrifying places that the internet could offer was that an establishment that hung the real thing on its walls instead of just prints didn't frighten her. Zac wouldn't have been afraid either.

The coffee lounge boasted widely spaced groups of tables. Very quiet, very discreet, and the waiters seemed to glide soundlessly across the thick carpet. Allie was shown to a door, which opened onto a beautifully furnished room, where Sir Anthony got quickly to his feet from a leather armchair.

'Dr Maitland-Hill. Thank you so much for taking the trouble to meet me.' Sir Anthony's soft Yorkshire accent, ready smile and rather crumpled appearance belied the real influence he wielded.

'I'm a little puzzled, Sir Anthony. What's this all about?'

'Straight to the point. Good.' Sir Anthony gave her a jovial smile and the waiter took her coat and her order for coffee. Sir Anthony instructed him to leave the door open, and waved her to one of the other armchairs around a highly polished coffee table.

'Little bit musty in here. I think some fresh air is in order.'

He was being tactful. Allie had written that, amongst many other things, closed doors in unfamiliar places made her fearful. She should start as she meant to go on, however challenging that felt.

'I appreciate the gesture, Sir Anthony. It doesn't seem musty in here to me.'

Sir Anthony laughed suddenly. 'No, it isn't, is it? A rather clumsy attempt on my part to put you at your ease. Perhaps you'll forgive me for asking you here as well. It's one of the Minister's favourite haunts, which gives me an entrée, and I wanted to talk to you in a more discreet atmosphere than the hospital provides.'

There were few secrets at a hospital. Allie had learned that to her cost. 'That's appreciated too. It's very nice here.'

'Yes, they pride themselves on *nice*. I'd like to talk to you about your website and the initiative that's already been set up at the hospital to do what we can to help those who've been affected by image-based sexual abuse. I'd be grateful for any observations you might have…'

Allie was walking so quickly along the street that people were actually moving out of her way. She needed the speed because her head was spinning.

Sir Anthony had been as down-to-earth as everyone said he was, and he seemed to know everything that went on at the hospital. Clearly the rumours of him turning up in the waiting room in A&E at midnight, or in the elderly care ward at visiting times, and sitting quietly, watching and talking to people weren't an exaggeration.

He'd also obviously read pretty much everything on her website, including the comments and the post she'd made last night, and he'd clearly put two and two together from the pictures on the site, throwing in a few very nice remarks about Zac's professionalism and the success of his tenure in Australia. His avuncular manner disguised a mind that was as sharp as a surgical blade.

Allie was aware of the initiative that had been set up at the hospital. She'd seen the posters and read the guidelines that had been provided for the care of both staff and patients. They'd all seemed a little too official for something that was so agonisingly personal, and she'd gravitated towards seeking help from survivor accounts. And that was what Sir Anthony had wanted to talk to her about.

He'd shared his own experience of horrified helplessness when he'd discovered that his own niece had been sharing personal images at school. He'd also offered Allie her own office and job title at the hospital and she'd turned him down, telling him that the contacts she'd made required a discreet and impartial listening ear from someone who'd been through the same as they had. Sir Anthony had understood, wondering if his own personal advocacy and support, along with his extensive list of contacts in the media, the health service and the judiciary might be of any assistance to her. It had taken a measure of self-control to stop herself from jumping to her feet and punching the air.

She was on her way. There was still a very long road ahead of her, but she had a powerful ally in Sir Anthony, and all of her instincts told her that he'd listen to what she and the other survivors wanted and come through on his promises.

All she wanted to do now was to call Zac. The one man who'd already come through on all of his promises, the man she'd walked away from because he'd been so adamant that it was the right thing to do. The man whose loss had hurt her more than anything else.

He'd know. Allie had to trust that, despite Zac's insistence on a clean break, he wouldn't let go of her so easily, and that he'd be keeping a close eye on her campaign. One of the good things about the internet… She'd already passed two Underground stations and it was time to stop walking and go home.

Walking down the steps into the busy, flood-lit station concourse, all Allie could think about was the open air and the warm feel of Zac's touch on her skin. And how much she missed him.

Zac was cradling Finn in his arms, under the shade of the large awning that stretched across one end of the patio. Mark was managing to combine keeping Izzy away from the heat of the barbecue with not burning the steaks, and Naomi was fetching the drinks.

'Any news from Allie?' he asked as Naomi put an ice-cold beer in a Surf City stubby holder in front of him.

'I asked you here to eat, Zac, not interrogate me. Remember eating? That thing you do to keep body and soul together.'

Zac ate. He surfed as well. Just not with the same enthusiasm he'd once shown.

'Interrogate is a bit of a harsh word.' He smiled at Naomi. He didn't do that with the same enthusiasm he'd once felt either.

'The cap fits, Zac.'

Fair enough. Zac knew that Naomi kept in touch with Allie, and his hunger for news of her wasn't slaked by reading through the website every evening. He supposed that asking Naomi if she'd had an email every time he saw her was overdoing it a bit.

'Why don't you just email her? You know

email? The thing that normal people do when they want to find out what's happening with someone?'

'She has to do this on her own. I can't interfere.'

'Granted. And she's doing it—she landed an interview on local radio the other day.'

Zac felt his ears prick. He hadn't heard about that. 'What station?'

'Some London station. I don't know.' Naomi rolled her eyes and then took pity on him. 'You want me to send you the link to the stream?'

'Yes please. Thank you.' Now would be good.

'I'll send it tonight. *After* we've eaten.' Naomi's attention was drawn to Izzy, who was pouring water over the chalk line on the patio, drawn at a safe distance from the barbecue.'

'Izzy! Rubbing out the line doesn't mean that Dad and I will forget it's there. You still can't cross it.'

Izzy stuck out her lower lip and took her half-full bucket back into the house, followed by Mark's watchful gaze.

Zac chuckled. 'Off to think of another way to cross the line?'

'Yeah, of course. She hasn't quite learned that however sneaky she can be, I can be sneakier.' Naomi turned her attention back to Zac. 'So what's the problem with just emailing Allie then? It's perfectly possible to let her get on with what she has to do and still make a civil enquiry about how she is, isn't it?'

'There were no hard feelings between us when she left.' Zac answered Naomi's implied question. 'The opposite, in fact.'

'Yeah, I noticed the part about the opposite. Zac, Allie's the best thing that ever happened to you.'

Grief squeezed at his heart, and Zac looked down at the child in his arms, wondering if Finn would wake up any time soon and give him the opportunity of a little mindless play. Thinking about things really didn't help.

'I know. We made a clean break. Going back to London was the right thing for Allie to do—the thing she needed to do. I just facilitated the one thing that would help her move forward.'

'I get that, and I know it was a difficult gesture for you to make. But honestly, Zac, it doesn't look like a very clean break to me. You've been miserable this last six weeks.'

Miserable was Zac's more positive face, the one he showed to the world. Naomi should see him when he was on his own.

'I made a promise.'

Naomi rolled her eyes. 'Yes, and you keep your promises, even when it's hard. That's a very commendable thing. But you see that child?' She nodded towards Finn. 'I'd break every rule, every promise I ever made for him and Izzy. And for Mark too, although if you ever tell him that you're toast.'

'I don't need to, do I?' Something ignited in Zac's chest. Hard, glittering, painful hope.

'I suppose not… Uh—hang on…' Naomi got to her feet, walking over to Izzy, who had just appeared from the kitchen, a plastic tumbler in her hand. Zac watched as Naomi bent down, putting her arm around Izzy's shoulders and whispering in her ear. The little girl nodded, and made her way over to Zac.

'Mum says that Dad doesn't need a drink, but you do, Uncle Zac.'

No doubt because he was on the right side of the chalk line. Zac leaned forward, taking the tumbler from her hand and gulping down the water.

'Just what I needed, Izzy, thank you.' The little girl nodded, clearly appeased, and Zac made room for her to climb up onto his lap, hugging her with his free arm.

'There you go.' Naomi walked back over to him, bending to plant a kiss on each of her children's heads. 'All my promises in one place.'

'Am I a promise, Uncle Zac?' Izzy snuggled against him.

'Course you are. Ask your mum about the

story of the Golden Promise.' Naomi seemed to have an endless ability to make up stories for her kids at the drop of a hat.

'Ah, yes! The Golden Promise.' Naomi shot him a look that plainly indicated he'd pay for this later, and embarked on the story.

Izzy was listening intently to her mother now, which left Zac a little space to think. He really did need to consider which promises needed to be broken.

Friday evening. On Monday it would be six weeks to the day since he'd seen Allie off at the airport. Zac tried not to indulge in sums like that, but when he was tired it was difficult to resist.

He walked up the steps to his apartment, glad to get home. Throwing his keys onto the breakfast bar and his bag onto the floor, he walked over to the sliding doors that overlooked the sea and then changed his mind. He didn't want to engage with the world at the moment, or at least not this side of it. Zac slumped down onto the long sofa, closing his eyes.

After a great deal of thought, he *had* emailed Allie, just two days ago. He'd told her that he read her blog still, and that he'd heard the several radio interviews she'd given, and that he was impressed with how much success she'd

had in so short a time. And then one short para-
graph, saying the things he regretted bitterly he
hadn't said at the airport. He treasured the time
they'd spent together, and wished her only love
and happiness.

He hadn't expected a reply, and had said as
much in his email. But he'd got one, written
while he'd slept and which he'd read the following morning. It hurt more than Zac had words to
describe. Allie had told him that she loved him.

It made everything so much harder. She'd said
that at the airport, even though they both knew
that she had to go. He'd almost hoped that she
didn't really mean it, or that *love* could be taken
in the context of the way that he loved Naomi
and Izzy, Mark and Finn. Wanting only the best
for them and being happy when they were, without needing them to be there on a daily basis.

He heard a knock at the door. Probably Naomi
with another food parcel. He was going to have
to make her coffee, sit her down and tell her that
tough love demanded she stop and make him
fend for himself. He'd go to the supermarket
tomorrow, and have them all round for lunch
on Sunday.

Naomi didn't burst straight in as she usually
did.

'It's open. You can come in, I'm decent...' He
hadn't yet got to the Friday evening, living-on-

his-own ritual of throwing off his work clothes, taking a shower and then padding around the apartment naked to cool off.

'That's a disappointment…'

Zac opened his eyes with a start.

Allie was standing in the open doorway. For a moment he thought that she must be a mirage, because she looked refreshed and awake. Zac tried to do the calculation regarding time differences, flight times and the amount of time it would take to look as fragrant and bright-eyed as Allie did, and failed miserably.

'Allie…? I thought you were in London.' That was unnecessary. She *had* been in London last week, when she'd given that radio interview. Hadn't she? In a world where suddenly everything was tipped upside down, anything was possible.

'I got your email on the morning before I left to come here.'

That was one mystery solved. Allie pressed her lips together in a half-frown, and he realised that she was waiting for him to invite her in.

'Come in. I'll make coffee…' She probably didn't need coffee after such a long flight. 'Or some juice. Where are you staying?'

'Naomi picked me up at the airport. I've been asleep in her spare room for most of the day.'

Second mystery solved. Zac couldn't bring

himself to ask about the third, agonisingly important one.

He walked to the kitchen, flipping on the coffee machine. If Allie didn't need coffee then he did. And he needed some way of keeping his eyes off her. She looked amazing, in a yellow sleeveless dress, her pale skin an enticing novelty in the heat of a Sydney summer.

'So...how's it all going?' He asked the question over his shoulder, pretending to fiddle with the coffee filter, and Allie came to sit down at the breakfast bar.

'It's good. I suppose you've heard from Naomi that I had an approach from Sir Anthony Greve, and he's been a big help in introducing me to people who can push for change and making sure that anyone who does want to come forward is treated with respect and cared for.'

'I...um...' Zac turned, wondering how he should put this.

'It's okay, Zac. Naomi told me you'd been asking, and I said that it was quite all right for her to answer any questions you had. I didn't want to put her on the spot.'

Zac studied the floor. 'I wasn't quite so considerate.'

'No, well, you didn't need to be. They're your friends, Zac, and they love you.'

That word again. In *that* context. Zac bit back his disappointment.

'Has anyone else come forward?'

'Yes. It turned out that the nurse at the hospital, who I was talking with when I was here, actually had a copy of the video that was made of her. I went with her to the police and as they had proof they were able to arrest the perpetrator very quickly. And that was a breakthrough, because he hadn't disposed of the phone he used for the group, and they were able to retrieve all of the numbers of the other members. We've managed to find other victims as well and to reach out to them...' Allie frowned and Zac saw her hand shake as she passed her fingers wearily over her eyes. 'Zac, this isn't important right now...'

'Yes. It's important. I want to know.' He gritted the words out. This was what he'd given Allie up for, and he needed to know.

'I meant...' Allie's breath seemed to catch in her throat and she looked down at her fingers, wound tightly together in her lap. Zac thought he saw tears in her eyes.

'What did you mean, Allie?' He spoke more gently this time.

'It's important but it's not why I'm here. You were right to say that I needed to leave, and that I could never forgive myself if I abandoned the people who'd contacted me. But we were both wrong too. I couldn't trust that I'd ever be able to heal enough to properly commit myself to you, and you couldn't believe that some promises can never be broken.'

'But I broke my promise to you, when I wrote that email.' Zac wasn't sure whether to apologise or tell her that he never should have committed himself in the first place.

'Yes, and I knew you were serious, because you don't break promises. That wasn't why I came back. I was already packed and was ready to leave. It did make the journey much easier, though.'

Maybe he should wait. Let Allie tell him exactly what she was here for and what she wanted of him. But Zac couldn't. He knew already, and it didn't need words. He strode around the breakfast bar, taking her hands in his.

'Allie, I love you. Maybe we needed this time apart to know that our relationship is stronger than anything that's happened in the past. But I know now that it is, and I want to be with you. You're the most important thing in my life, and we can work something out. I don't know how, but...'

A tear rolled down her cheek. A happy one, because Allie was smiling. 'We don't need to work anything out. When I first went back to

London, Sir Anthony offered me a job and I turned it down. But I've done everything I can working alone, and now he's talking about setting up a joint venture with the hospital here in Australia, to help patients like Carly and their families and to reach out into local communities and on the web. I've agreed to head it up, as long as I get the choice of working either here or in London. If I come here, he'll arrange my work permit—'

She could stop talking now. Zac kissed her and she flung her arms around his neck.

'I love you.' He whispered the words, planting a kiss on her neck

'I love you too, Zac.'

'Will you marry me?'

Allie squealed with delight, kissing him again. 'Yes, Zac. I'll marry you.'

No more words needed. No plans because they'd just made the one and only plan that they needed to. Everything else would fall into place around that.

EPILOGUE

Five months later...

ZAC AND ALLIE's summer together in Sydney had contained so many days that were perfect. But this had been the best of all. They'd been married at a joyous informal ceremony at one of the lookout points above Sydney Harbour, surrounded by friends and colleagues. Allie's mum and dad had made the journey to be here, and even Sir Anthony had altered the timing of a planned visit to the hospital in Sydney so that he could attend. When she'd looked into Zac's eyes to say her vows she knew that he heard her promises and that she knew they'd never be broken.

The reception was held in the shade of massive trees, an afternoon full of love and plans for the future. Carly was there, having agreed to act as the official wedding photographer, and although she still preferred to stay behind the camera rather than in front of it her photography had taken on a new dimension. She and Allie had talked a lot about the relationship that formed across a camera lens, and that had informed her work. She was making her way back to being a young artist full of promise, whose photographs truly portrayed the people framed within them.

As the sun began to fall in the sky there were kisses and farewells. One last toast, and then it was time for Allie and Zac to leave. They would spend one night by the beach—their beach—in Cronulla and then drive to the cabin in the Blue Mountains the following morning for their honeymoon.

'You're sure about this?' Zac asked as they stood on the balcony of their apartment, surrounded by the sounds of the sea. 'It's such a beautiful dress, and you could always wear it again...'

Allie had decided on a light dress, trimmed with cotton lace, to suit the informality of the day. Zac's cream linen suit, worn with an open-necked shirt, matched the tone perfectly too.

'I suppose so. But this dress was always just for today, Zac.'

He smiled down at her. 'Because our memories of today will always be fresh. Never yellowed with age, or stained, or torn.'

'Don't you like the idea?'

He took her in his arms, kissing her. It seemed that neither of them could get enough of each other's kisses today. 'I love it. I just wanted to make sure that you hadn't changed your mind.'

'I'll never change my mind about anything we've done today.'

Zac chuckled. 'Me neither. I'll meet you on the beach?' He kissed her again, as if parting for only five minutes was far too much to bear, and then shooshed her up the stairs.

The first red streaks were beginning to appear in the sky, and they had the beach to themselves now. Mark was clearly taking his best man duties seriously, and was lounging in a fold-up chair at the top of the beach, flipping through a surfing magazine, while Zac waited at the water's edge.

'You're still keeping an eye on Zac?' Allie grinned at Mark.

'Someone's got to. As well as unobtrusive lifeguard and clearing up duties so we don't contribute to the marine litter situation. And since Naomi's busy putting the kids to bed I'm deputising as matron of honour. Your hair and your dress look absolutely fine.'

Allie chuckled. 'Great job, Mark. Covering all the bases.'

'So you're going to do it, then? Trash the dress?'

'No! This is my way of keeping it, just as it is. My special dress for one day only.'

'Not really as catchy,' Mark observed dryly. 'You'd better get on with it then, before it gets dark. Your husband's right there...'

And Allie couldn't get to him fast enough. The man she'd always love, waiting for her on the beach, his trouser legs rolled up and the evening breeze tugging at his shirt. She savoured the moment though, resisting the temptation to run into Zac's arms in favour of walking towards him.

'That's a picture I'll keep.' He smiled at her. 'My wife, barefoot on the beach, in a white dress.'

Allie laughed. 'And my husband, waiting for me in the sunset...'

The two-person paddleboard was already inflated, and Zac picked it up, wading with it into the water. Allie gathered her dress up around her knees and got onto the board, sitting down so that Zac could paddle them out. Alone at last amongst the quiet swell of the waves, Zac took her hand, steadying her as she got to her feet.

'Ready?' He grinned at her.

'I'm ready.' Before he could ask her again

whether she really wanted to do this, Allie jumped into the water, taking Zac with her.

The feeling of leaping into the unknown with him, knowing that he'd be there always, was exhilarating. But as Allie hit the water the dress became tangled around her legs and it was only Zac's arm around her waist that kept her afloat.

'Oh! This is more complicated than I'd anticipated.'

'You're doing fine.' Zac kissed her and she felt herself melt against him.

'Hang onto me while I get the buttons…' Allie grimaced. The row of small buttons down the back of the dress were going to be fiddly.

'No need. Put your arms around my neck…' Zac reached up onto the paddleboard, flipping open the box that was secured to the back of it and withdrawing a button hook. 'I came prepared.'

He supported her in the water, one arm holding onto the side of the paddleboard, the other behind her back. He'd clearly been practising how to do this and the hook made short work of the buttons. Then Allie floated in his arms while she undid the buttons at her cuffs.

'I've just got to get it over my head now.' Now that the dress was waterlogged that seemed a little more difficult than she'd thought it might be.

'That's okay. Hold onto the board.'

Allie grabbed the board, feeling his hand slide up her leg. 'Zac! Stop messing around.'

'I'm your husband. Isn't that part of the job?'

Allie kissed him. 'It's definitely part of the job. Later…'

'I'll look forward to it.' He disappeared under the water, swimming around her legs, and the dress blossomed around her as he folded it upwards. When he surfaced, taking hold of her cuff, Allie found that she could get her free arm out of the dress easily.

'One more thing and you're out.' He held her against him, and Allie wrapped her legs around his waist. She could lift the dress over her head now, leaving just the white swimming costume she wore underneath it.

'Am I going to get to undress you now?'

He grinned. 'Later. You could undo my shirt if you wanted…'

Allie didn't need to be asked twice and she tugged at the buttons on his shirt. There was an unfamiliar chain around his neck and Zac was grinning.

'What's this?' She followed the chain with her finger. 'A key! Does this mean we have a front door to go with it?'

'A back door as well. And windows.'

'Zac!' Allie flung her arms around his neck.

'Our beautiful new house has doors and windows!'

'Yes, and that's your key. I had your initials engraved on it. AF.'

'That's so sweet!' Allie inspected the engraving on the key, her new initials surrounded by a heart. Zac pulled the chain over his head, putting it around her neck.

'While we're on our honeymoon the plasterers will be going in and then they'll start laying the floors and fitting the kitchen. Mark said he'd keep an eye on it all while we're away, and with any luck we'll be able to move in, in a couple of months.'

A wedding. A house built overlooking the sea in Cronulla. And maybe, after spending two weeks in a log cabin in the Blue Mountains…

'I'm working on keeping all of my promises, Allie.' He seemed to know what she was thinking. Zac had promised they'd have a family and she knew it was what he wanted. His childhood might have given him no idea of what it was like to have two supportive and loving parents, but he was writing his own script now. Zac was going to be a great dad.

'And I'm working on mine.' Allie had promised Zac that she would never give up on regaining her own space. She'd made a lot of progress with her counsellor, and worked hard to make the new joint initiative, sponsored by the Sydney and London hospitals, a success. Helping others who'd been hurt the way she had was hard, but it gave her a sense of deep satisfaction.

She watched as Zac launched himself backwards in the water, easing out of his shirt and trousers, to reveal a pair of board shorts. Then he hoisted himself onto the paddleboard and stretched out his hand to help Allie climb up with him.

'No regrets?' Zac nodded towards their wet clothes, piled beside her in a tangle of fabric and seaweed.

'Not one.'

'Me neither' He grinned, reaching into the box again and drawing out a bottle of champagne, two plastic beakers and a foil-wrapped package. 'Can I interest you in a few leftovers? Champagne and wedding cake?'

'Oh! Yes please. I was far too happy to eat or drink much this afternoon...'

'I noticed. So did your mum and she wrapped a couple of pieces and slipped them to me as we were leaving.'

Zac handed her the cake and Allie unwrapped it, while he popped the cork of the champagne bottle and poured a splash into each of their beakers.

They watched the sun go down on their wedding day, and then, as the warm breeze began to cool a little, Zac wrapped a fleece jacket around her shoulders and paddled them back to the shore.

They walked back to their apartment, hand in hand.

'The first day of our marriage. Thank you so much for making it perfect, Zac.'

He leaned over, kissing her. 'I have a feeling it's only going to get better. I can't wait to find out everything we'll do together.'

* * * * *